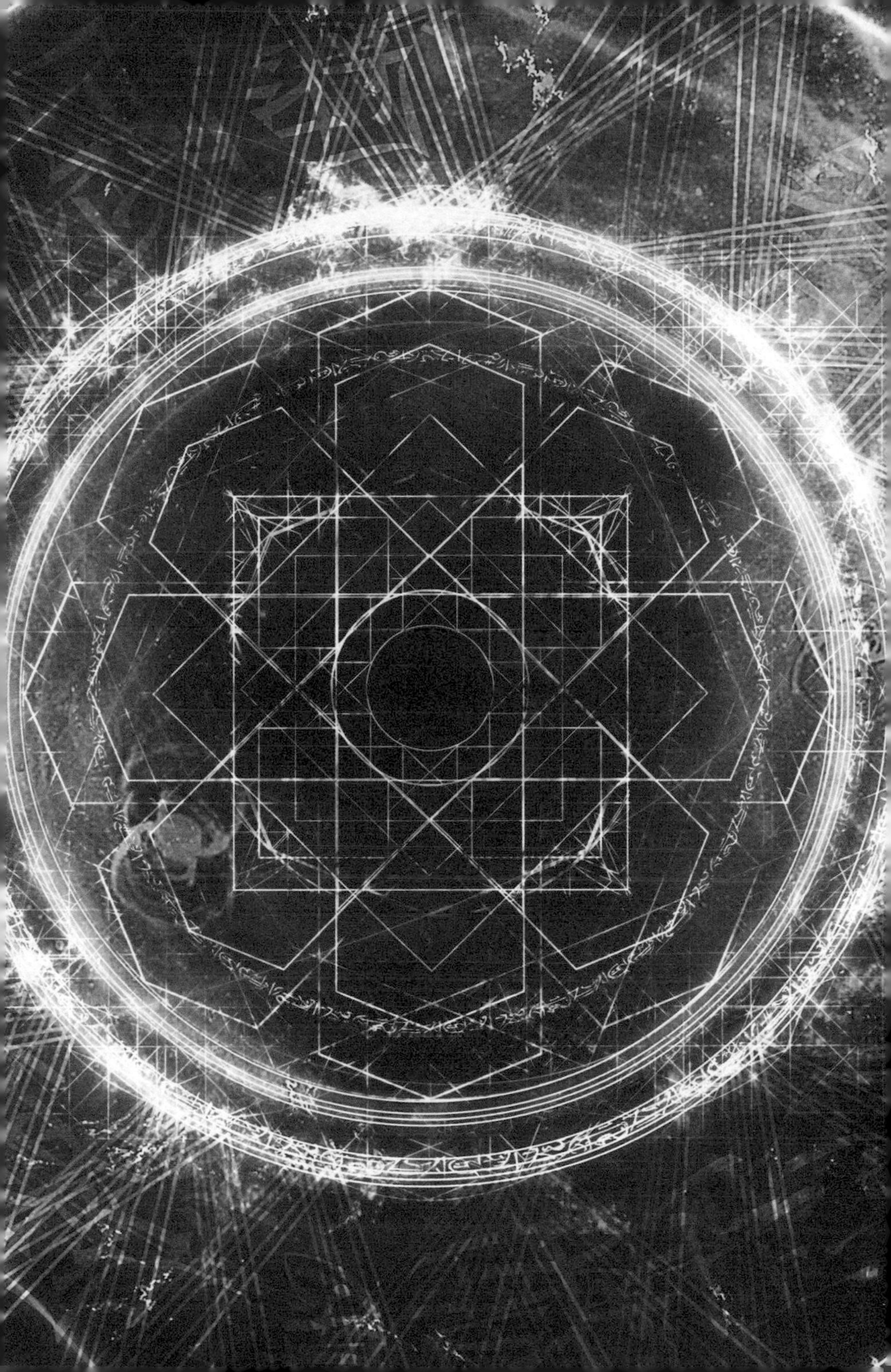

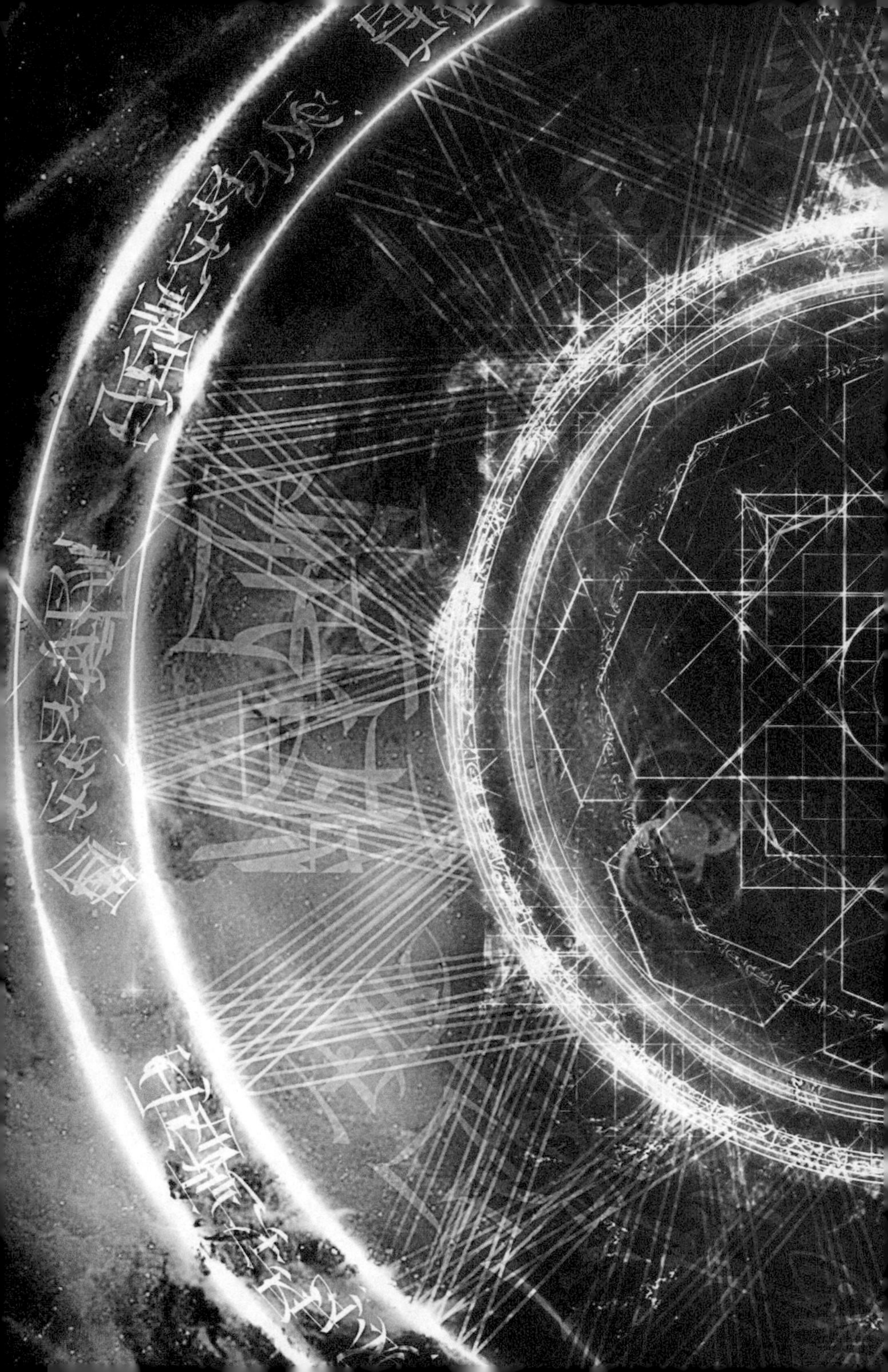

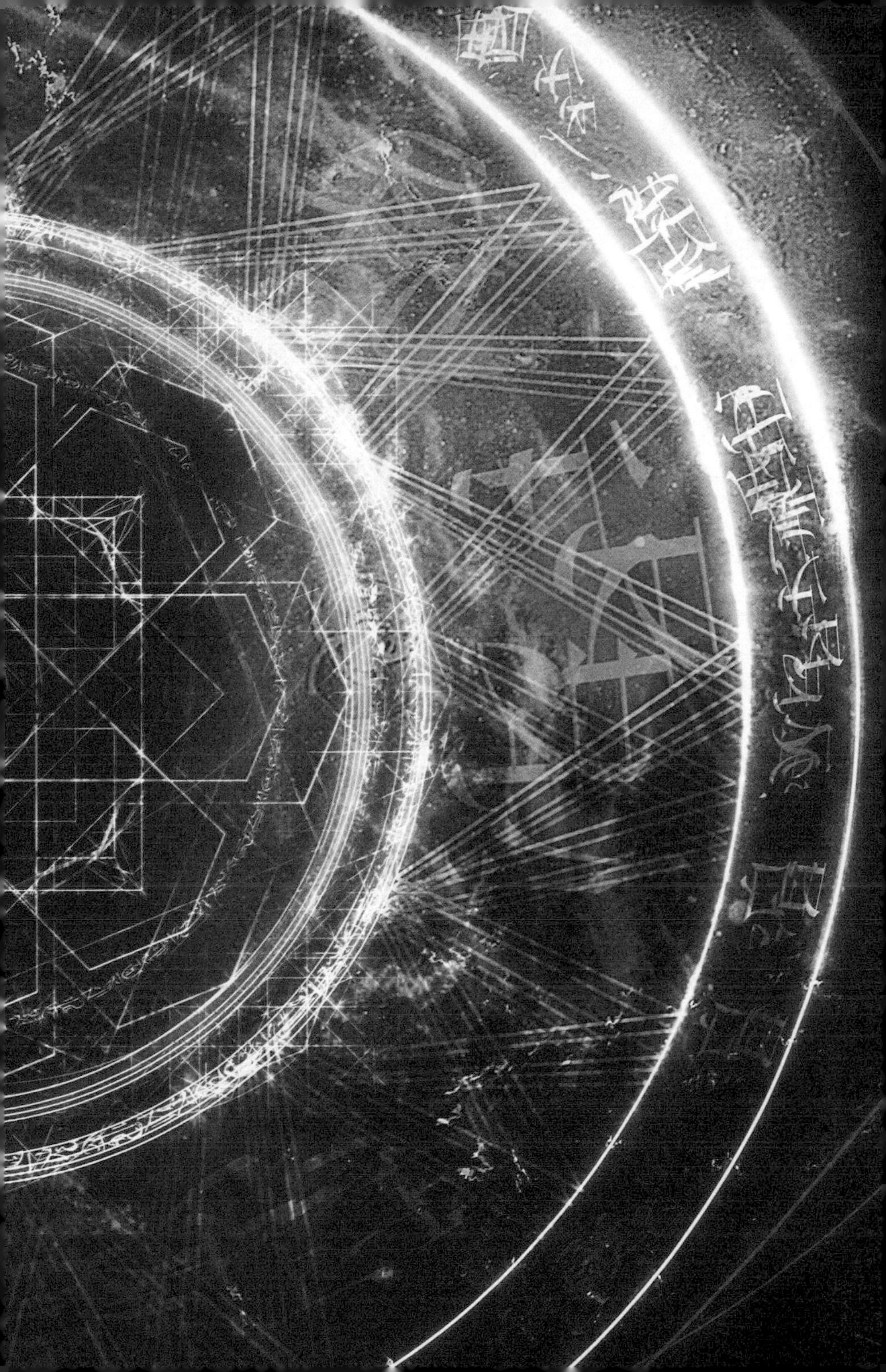

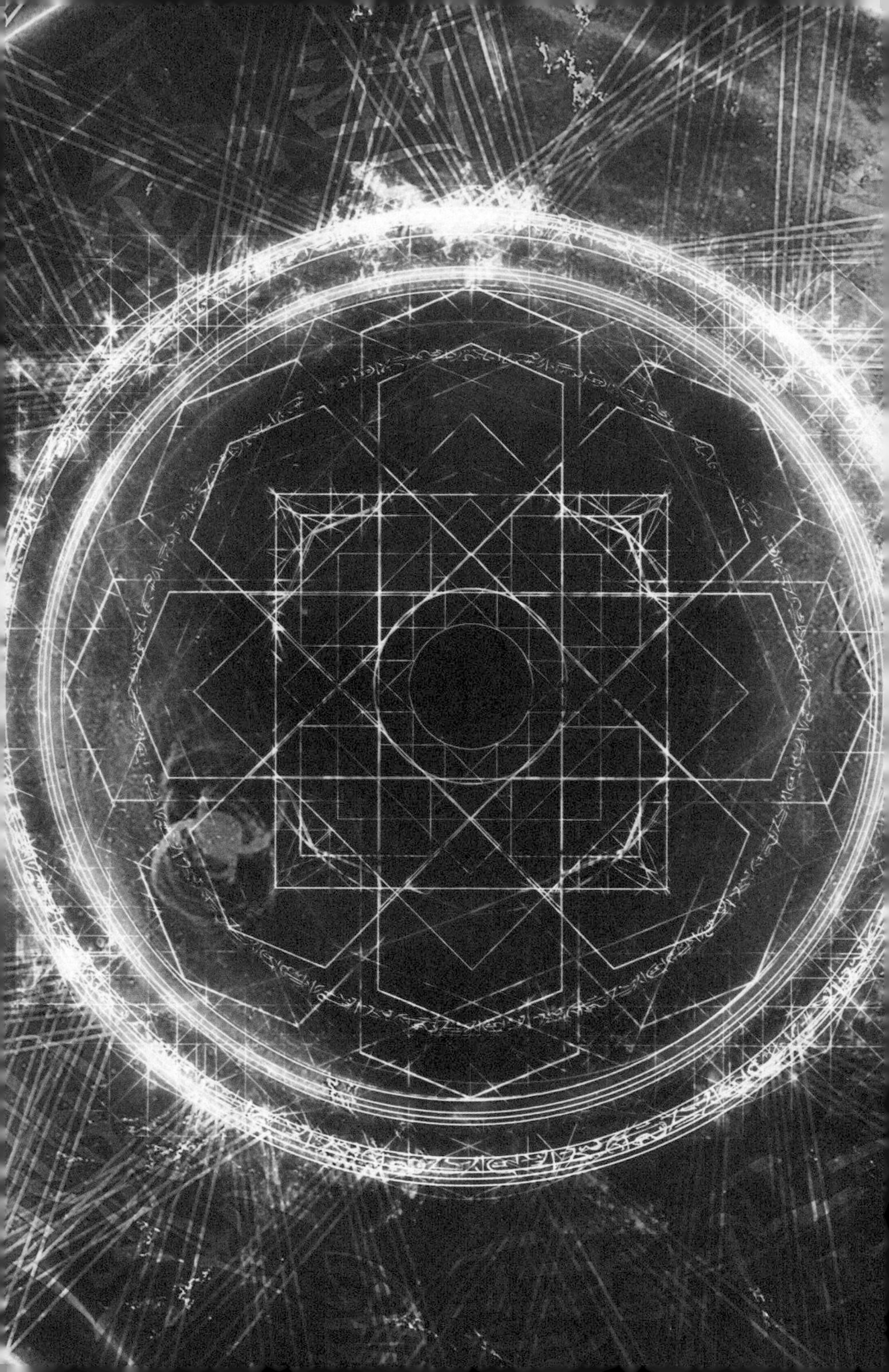

MARVEL

DOCTOR STRANGE

Strange Tales and Talismans

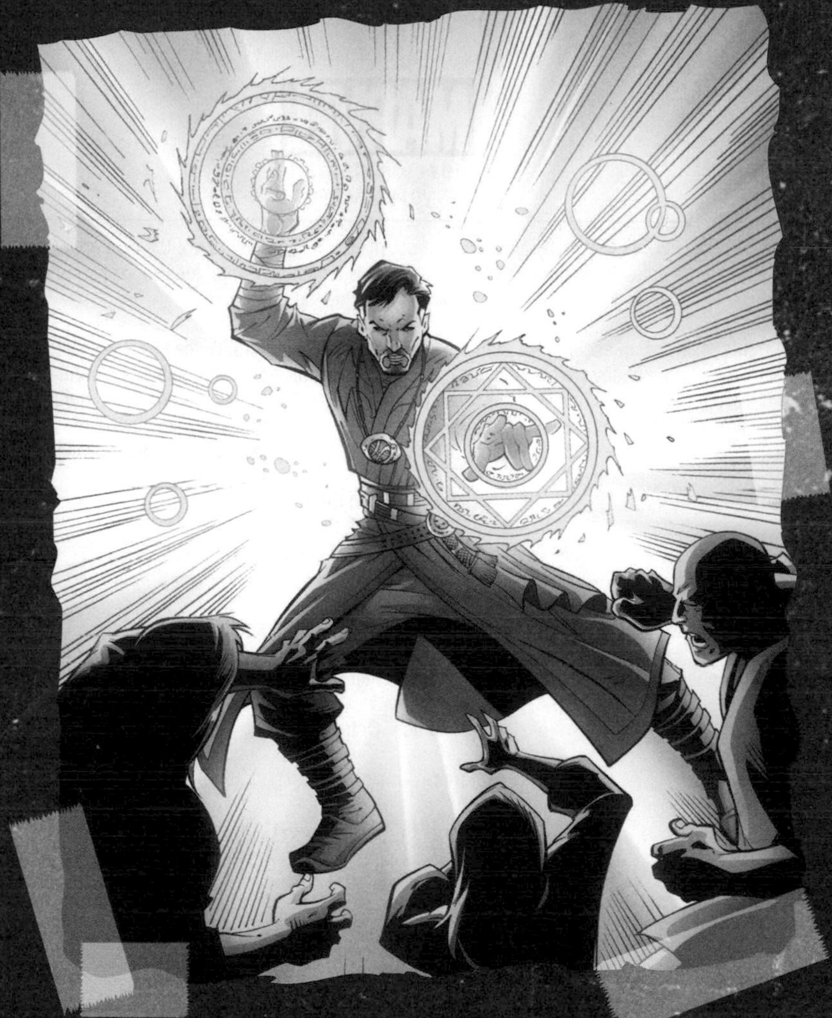

marvelkids.com
© 2016 MARVEL.

Little, Brown and Company
Hachette Book Group
1290 Avenue of the Americas, New York, NY 10104
Visit us at lb-kids.com

Little, Brown and Company is a division of Hachette Book Group, Inc.
The Little, Brown name and logo are trademarks of Hachette Book Group, Inc.
The publisher is not responsible for websites (or their content) that are not owned by the publisher.

First Edition: October 2016

Library of Congress Control Number: 2016949442

ISBN 978-0-316-27156-1

10 9 8 7 6 5 4 3 2 1

WOR

Printed in the United States of America

MARVEL

DOCTOR STRANGE

Strange Tales and Talismans

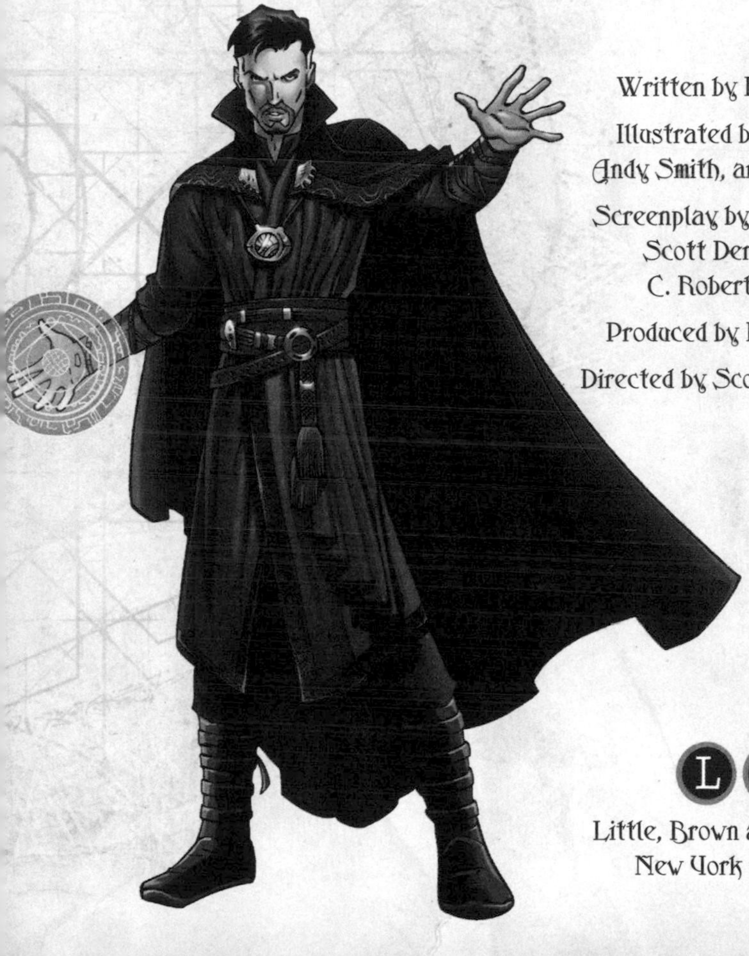

Written by R.R. Busse

Illustrated by Ron Lim, Andy Smith, and Andy Troy

Screenplay by Jon Spaihts, Scott Derrickson, C. Robert Cargill

Produced by Kevin Feige

Directed by Scott Derrickson

LB

Little, Brown and Company
New York • Boston

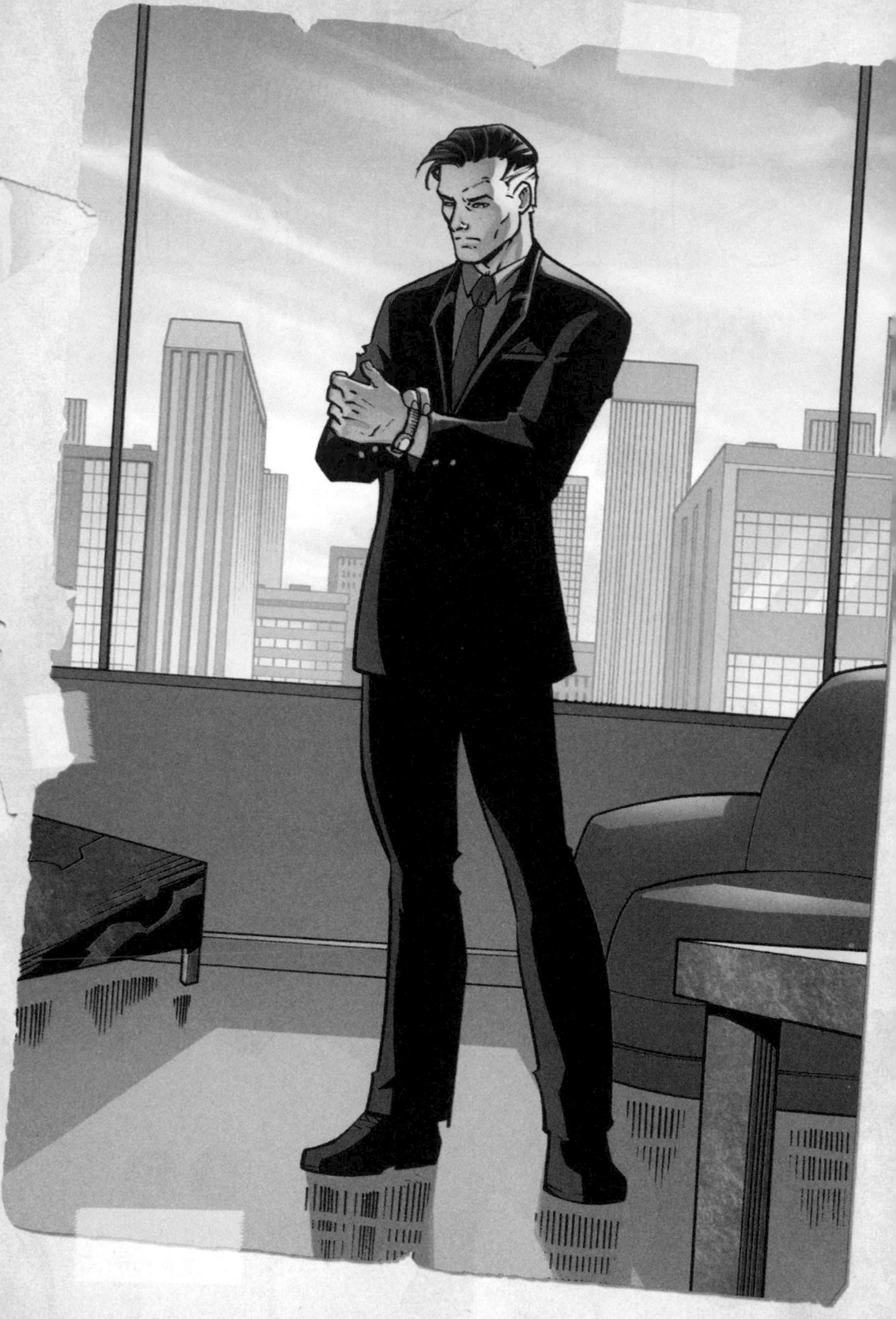

To Whom It May Concern:

What follows is the account of Doctor Stephen Strange, as it has been told to the Kamar-Taj historians. After his now-famous adventures and accomplishments, it was decided to create a permanent record of his origins for future scholars' study.

Apologies—the drawings included were done after the fact, and from the doctor's memory, so small details may be misplaced or incorrect. Because he was obviously in a rush through much of the following story, much of it was told as an overview.

Regards,
The Kamar-Taj Historical Society

ONE

Once upon a time, Doctor Stephen Strange was a skilled surgeon. There is a complicated ranking system for skilled surgeons, but at the time he would say that he was the greatest surgeon he had ever encountered, in any specialty. Some of Strange's friends and acquaintances openly wished he would tone down his bravado, but what did their opinions mean to someone as talented and sure of himself as Strange?

He worked in this → hospital for most of his career, showing aptitude and problem-solving skills other doctors surely envied, as he gained fame and fortune with one successful operation after the next.

DOCTOR STEPHEN STRANGE'S APARTMENT

Life was simple and very good to him. He had the finest clothes, a luxurious apartment, and a very fast car. He was Doctor Stephen Strange:

Winner at Life.

TWO

Then everything changed in an instant. The below shows him as he was driving on his way to a very important conference. He was going to be the keynote speaker, and in his mind he was positive that literally everyone was looking forward to it.

Normally, he was a competent driver. But that day, everything went wrong. Between the rain, his inability to find any good music on the radio, and an urgent call from work, he lost control of his car and wound up like this ➔

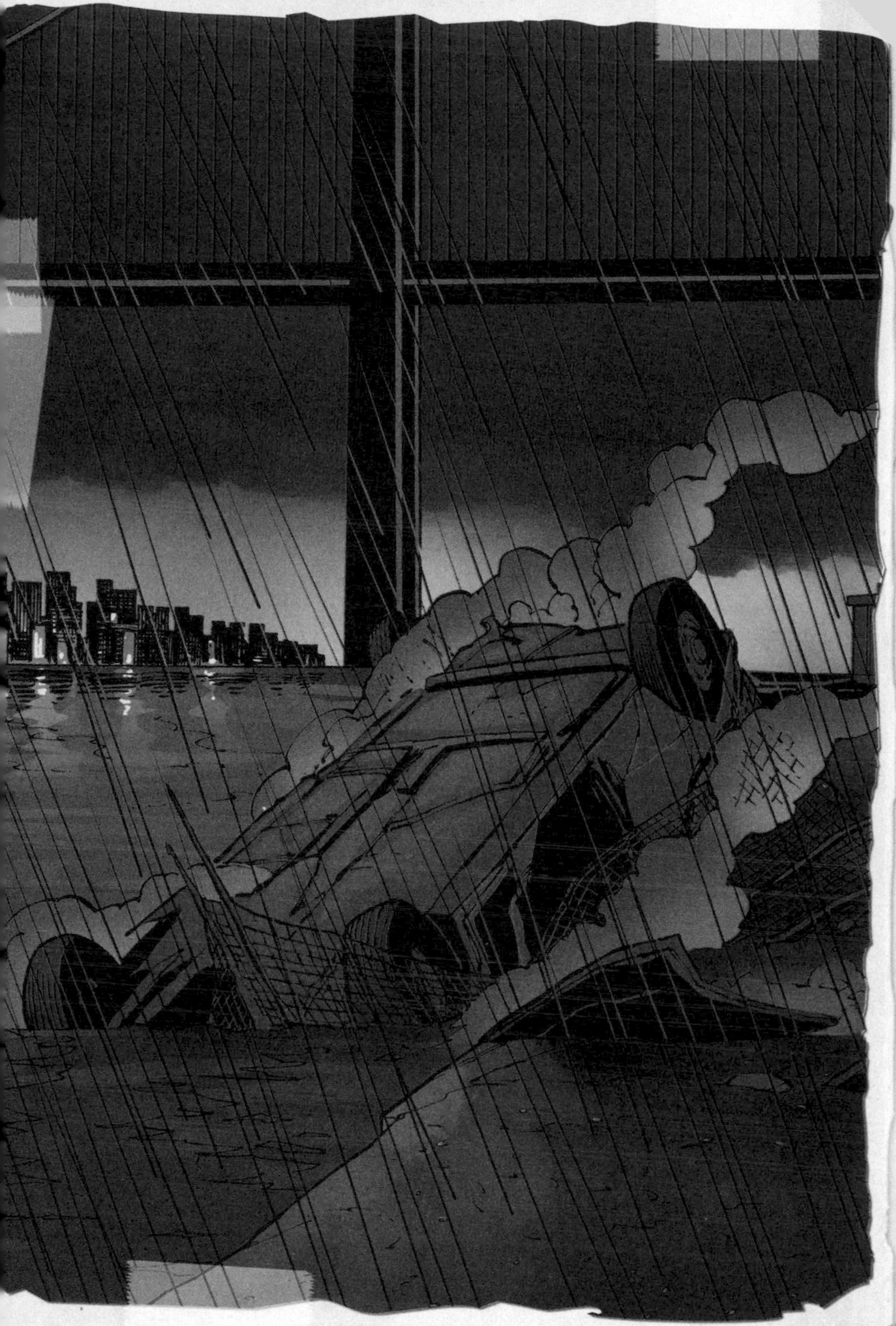

It was the beginning of a very dark time for Stephen Strange. That accident sent him on his adventure of self-discovery, which eventually brought him to Kamar-Taj.

He doesn't remember much about the crash itself, and can't speak to it. He heard metal screeching and felt a lot of water around him. And then...pain. And confusion. And more pain. His good friend Doctor Christine Palmer told him the staff at the hospital did everything they could to save him.

He looked like this:

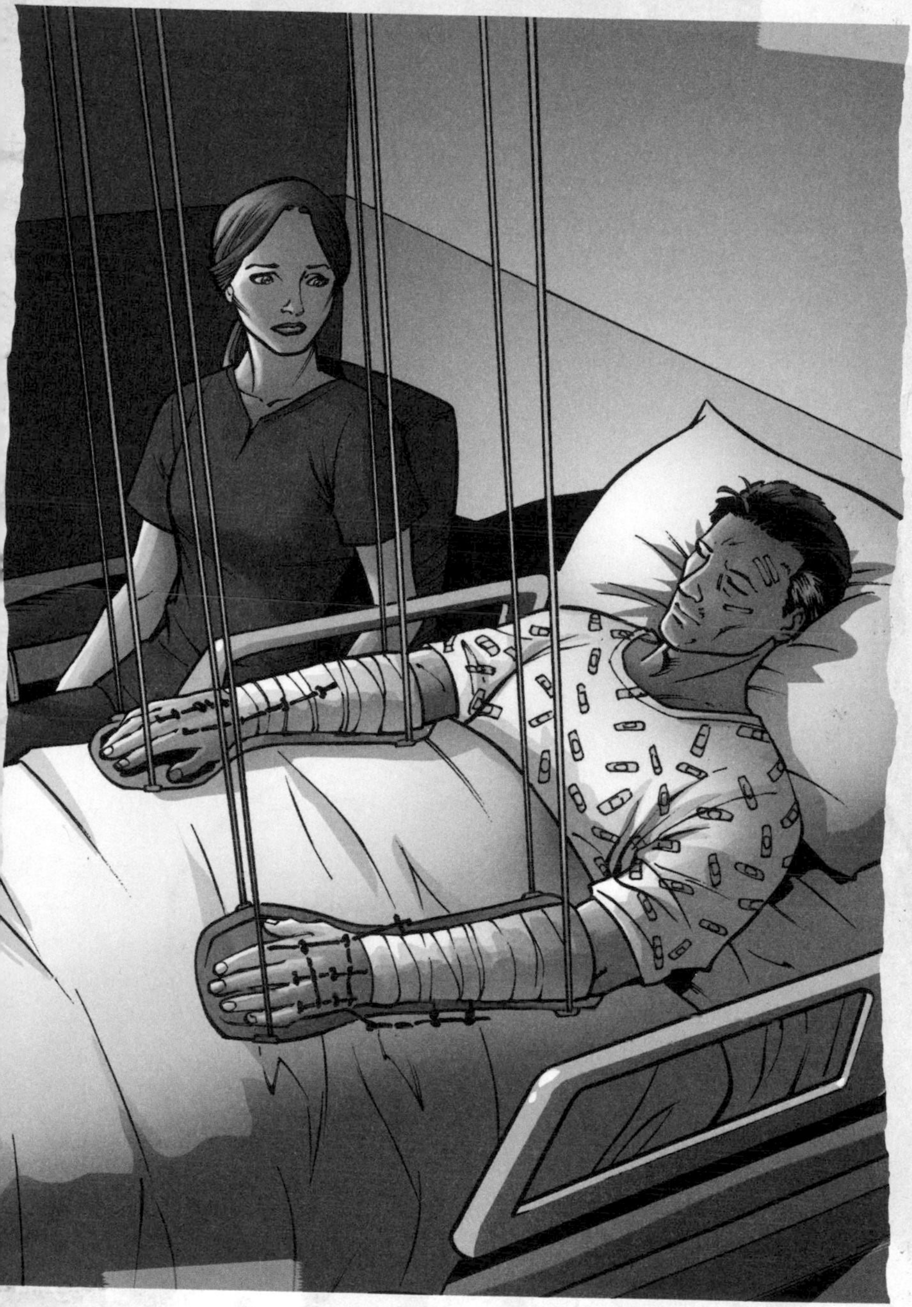

In his retelling, Strange would want to point out here that if he were the surgeon operating on himself, he believes that he would have been able to pull off the procedure as a complete success with none of the residual nerve damage that his "esteemed colleagues" left him with.

But he couldn't operate, obviously. His hands were left as shells of their former selves. Have you ever tried to hold something relatively light in one hand for as long as you can? Arm outstretched, you're eventually struggling to complete a simple task. And then your hand starts to shake. Uncontrollably. Uncomfortably. Unavoidably.

His hands had that feeling. All the time.

He couldn't function, and he certainly couldn't perform surgery anymore. He was at a professional, personal, and spiritual loss. He describes it as a very charming mixture of anger and despair. He was in a bad place, and didn't want to talk to anyone who couldn't fix his hands and give him his life back.

He was alone...

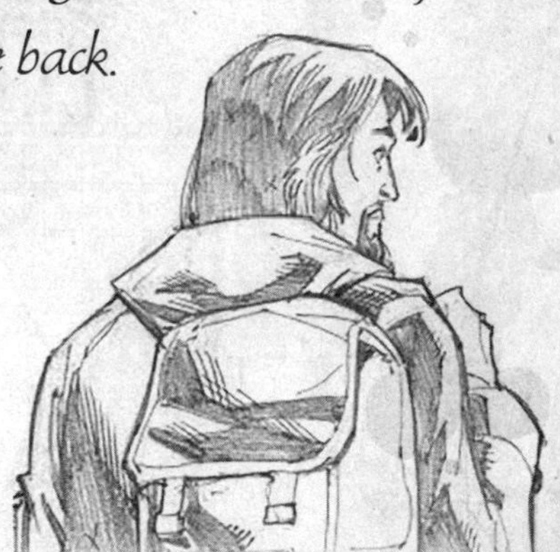

THREE

...until he talked to this man:

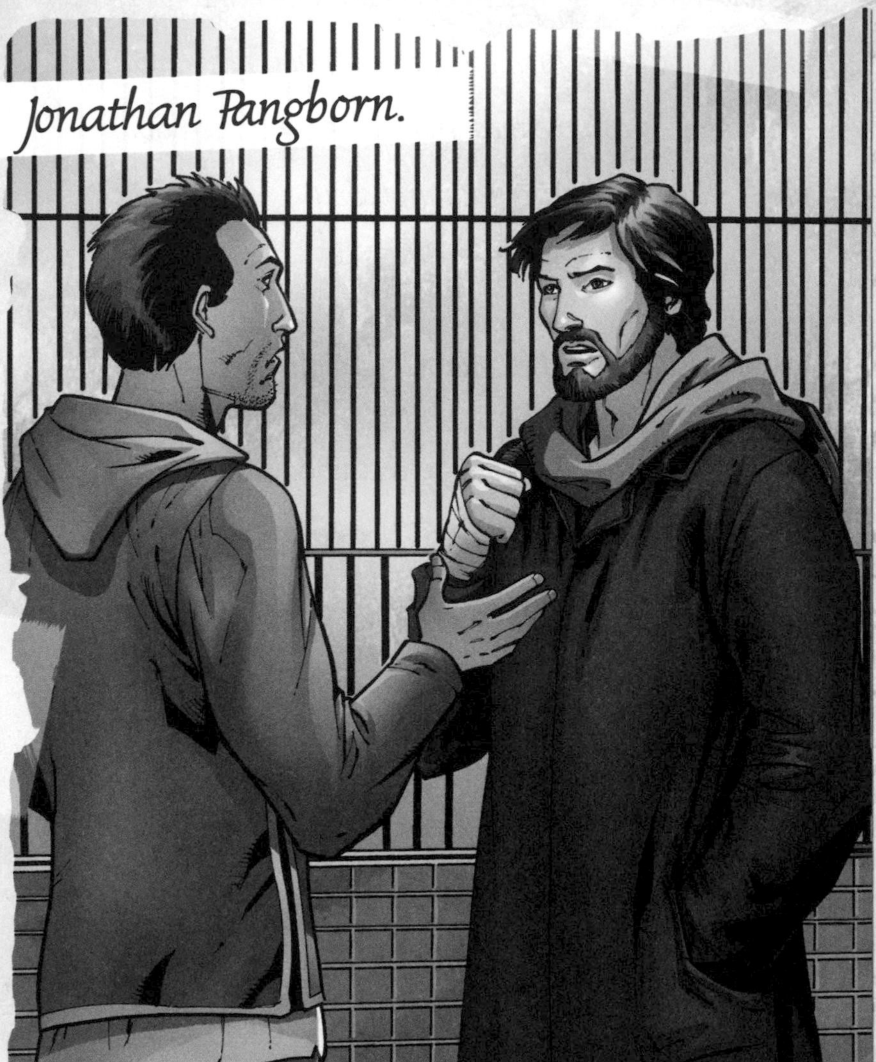
Jonathan Pangborn.

Sure, Pangborn didn't look like much. But Stephen is the first to admit, at this point neither did he. Would you believe that only a short time prior, Jonathan's spinal injury was so severe that even Stephen didn't believe himself capable of fixing it? Pangborn had been paralyzed from the mid-chest down, with partial paralysis in both hands. But Strange had heard from a friend that Mister Pangborn wasn't hampered at all anymore.

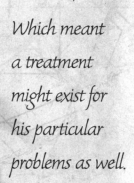

Which meant a treatment might exist for his particular problems as well.

Which ultimately meant that Doctor Stephen Strange searched for Jonathan Pangborn for weeks before he was finally able to speak to him.

Their conversation didn't exactly end on the best of terms, but Pangborn told Stephen a story about a place where he could learn how to elevate his mind, in the hopes that healing might follow.

Jonathan gave Strange the name, and nothing else:

Kamar-Taj.

FOUR

So Strange made the necessary preparations and left in search of a place he wasn't even sure really existed. He was desperate to find anything at all that could help him.

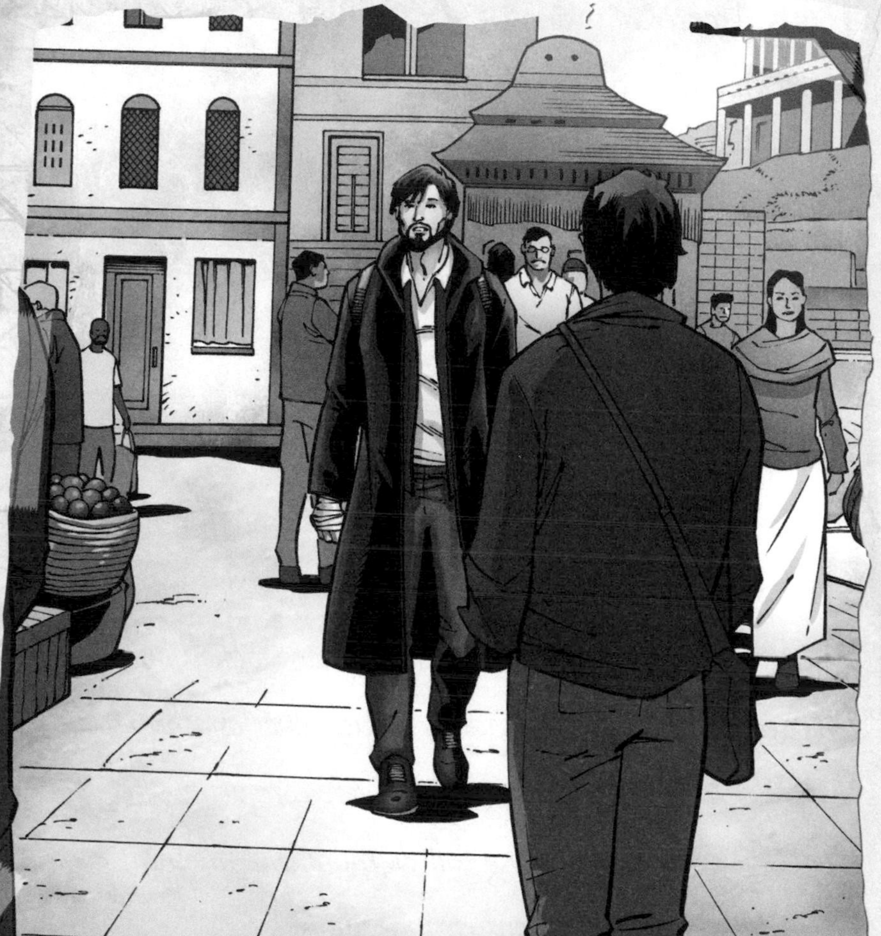

Soon he found himself in the city of Kathmandu. Which, to him, looked like any other generic urban center hawking false promises of enlightenment and healing to rubes with too much money and not enough common sense.

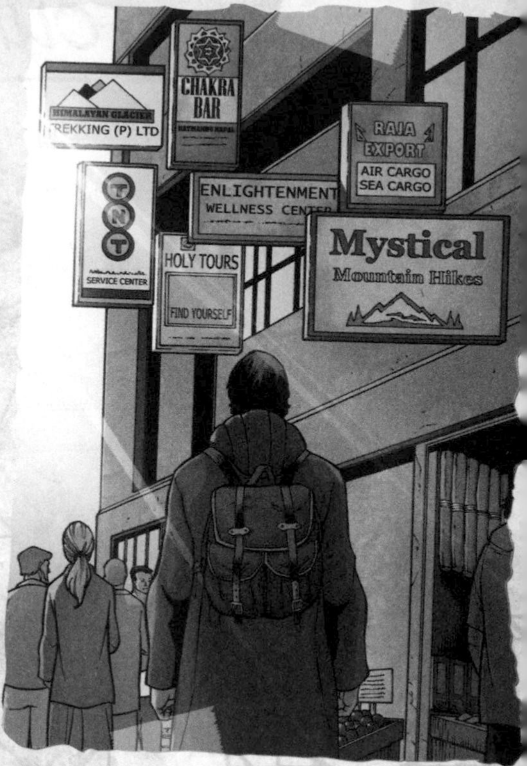

HIMALAYAN GLACIER
TREKKING (P) LTD
CHAKRA BAR
RAJA EXPORT
AIR CARGO
SEA CARGO
TNT
SERVICE CENTER
ENLIGHTENMENT
WELLNESS
HOLY TOURS
FIND YOURSELF
Mystical
Mountain Hikes

Even if there was some diamond in the rough among the shops and chakra bars (which he wasn't certain were a real thing), nothing around him looked like it would be able to provide a miracle like Jonathan Pangborn's. And although they were comforting, he felt he needed something a little more extreme than traditional Buddhist prayer wheels.

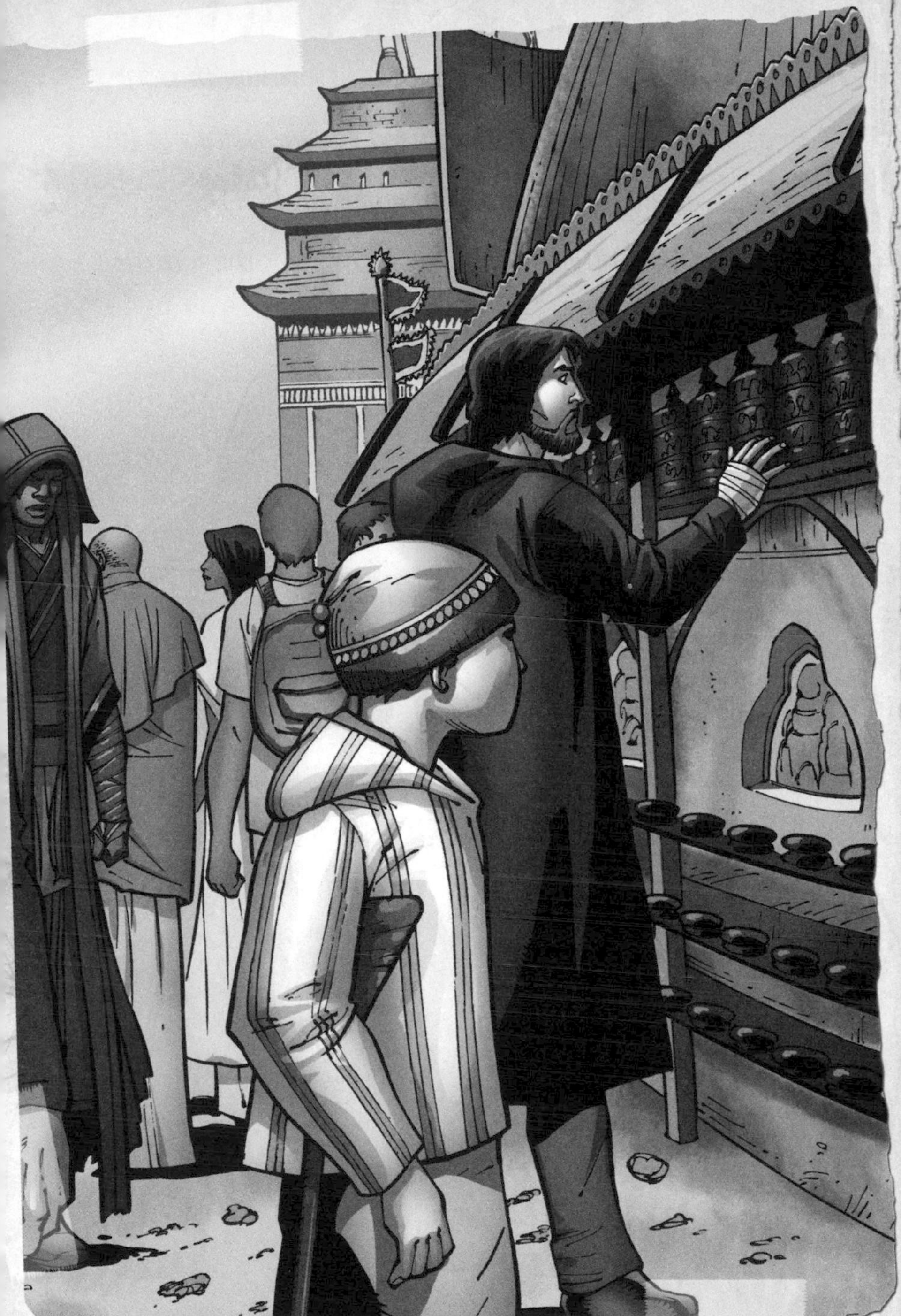

As he went through and recapped his journey thus far to us, Doctor Strange felt the need to add details to his story that he didn't necessarily know at the time, but were **definitely** there. One such example is the inclusion of the child and man in the green robes in the picture prior and to the right. Both would be important, but at the time Stephen didn't give either a second glance....

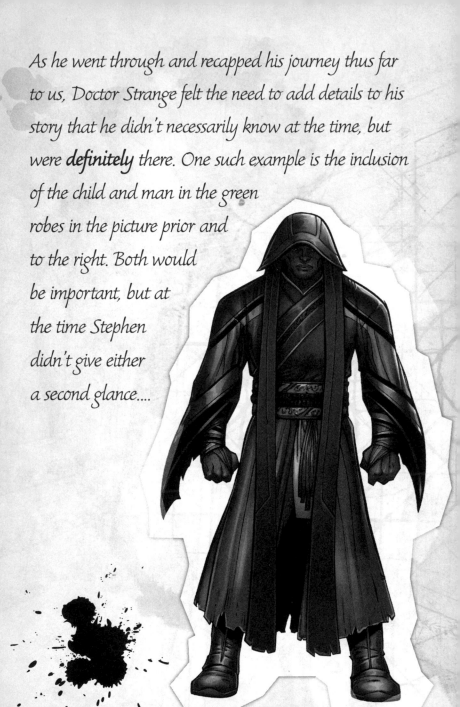

FIVE

After a bit of haggling and, by his own admission, bribing the kid with his last dollar, the child was kind enough to point Stephen in the vague direction of Kamar-Taj. While it wasn't what he would call exceedingly helpful, it did give him some hope that this place actually existed.

You'll notice that the man in green is closer here. In Strange's mind, the mysterious man **must** have always been there, but he has no earthly idea just how close the man got without him noticing anything. Strange sometimes looks back and wonders how he could ever be so oblivious.

SIX

One creature that ***wasn't*** *oblivious was a stray dog that came up to Strange, simply looking for a bit of food:*

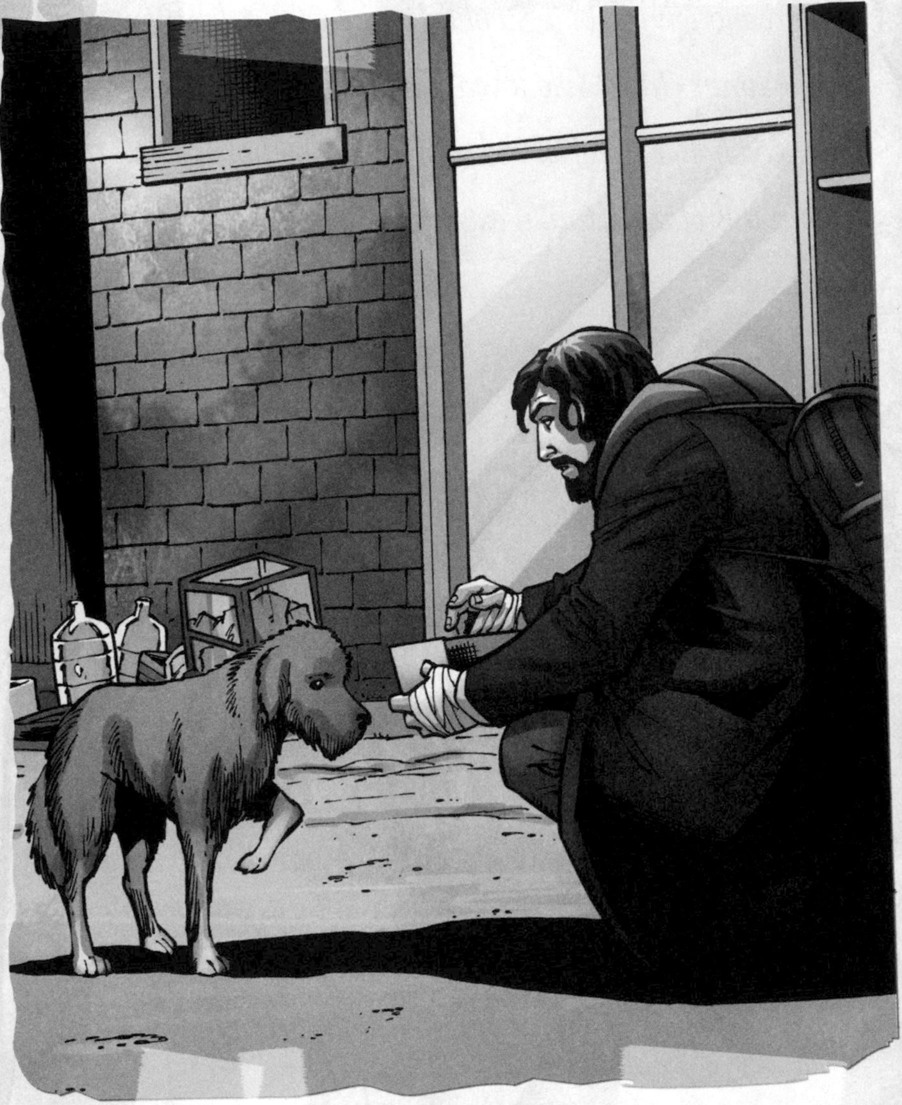

While he was trying to offer it some scraps that he had saved, Strange noticed the dog had hurt its paw. He wasn't a world-renowned surgeon anymore, but he was still able to splint its paw and give it a shot at survival on the streets. And he'd like to think that it was that small act of kindness that started the next and greatest portion of his journey—either through karma or fate, or just that man in green having a soft spot for dogs.

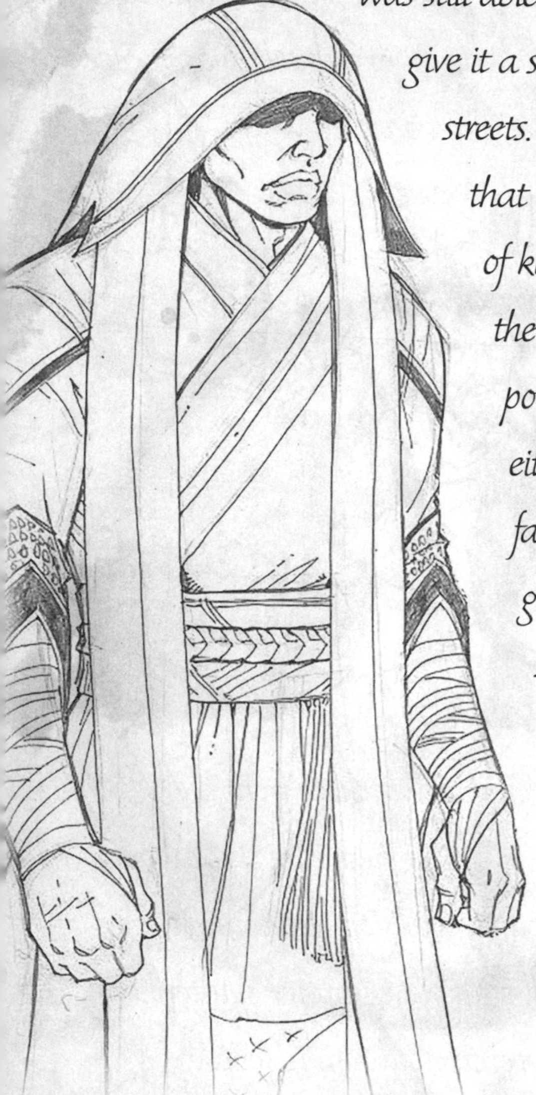

Soon after, he found himself set upon by a group of thieves, who were incredibly insistent on helping themselves to his watch. That watch was the last thing of value he owned at that point, and a precious reminder of the life he used to have. He unfortunately wasn't able to convince the men to let him go on his way.

Luckily, the man in green was watching from the background as always. In a blur, he made short work of the gang Strange thought was going to commit murder for a watch. All of this left Strange sputtering and helpless as the newcomer told him to follow.

SEVEN

KAMAR-TAJ!

The man in green was named Mordo and, after saving Stephen's life (and watch), agreed to take him to the mystical place he had nearly given up hope on.

The first thing Stephen noticed was the people training in a massive courtyard. Some were practicing martial arts, and some were meditating—everything he would have expected from an ancient and secret mystical city. But to his surprise he also saw some reading on cutting-edge tablets, or listening to music through headphones. This was going to be a different journey than he imagined when he set out.

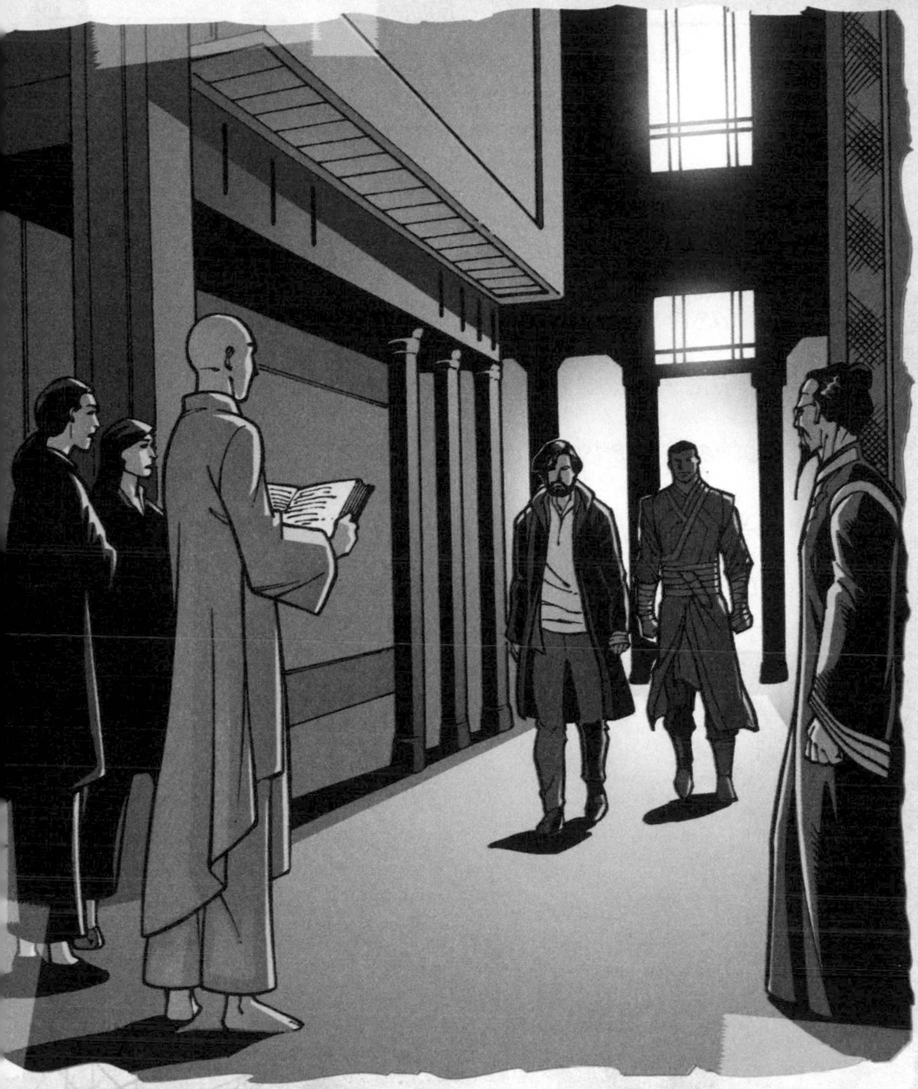

*Mordo soon brought Strange to meet **his** teacher, called The Ancient One. Silly name aside, Stephen was eager to meet the person he had traveled all over the world to find.*

EIGHT

That first meeting was, in Strange's words, well beyond weird, and frankly didn't start off on a high note. It turns out that as a man of science, he had a hard time believing in what The Ancient One was selling. She kept talking about other dimensions and opening his perception and all sorts of hokey-sounding mumbo-jumbo. He was ready to leave. But then, she **showed** him.

And Mordo **showed** him.

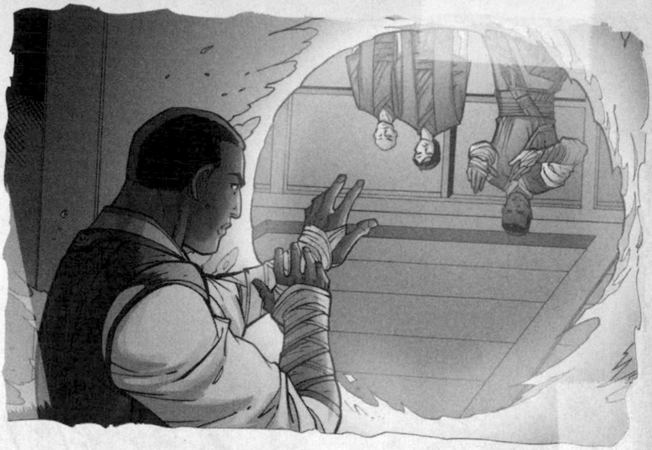

In fact, that first day, they showed him more than he ever could have imagined. It turned out that Doctor Stephen Strange, arguably the best former surgeon on the planet, was wrong about the world. Very, very wrong.

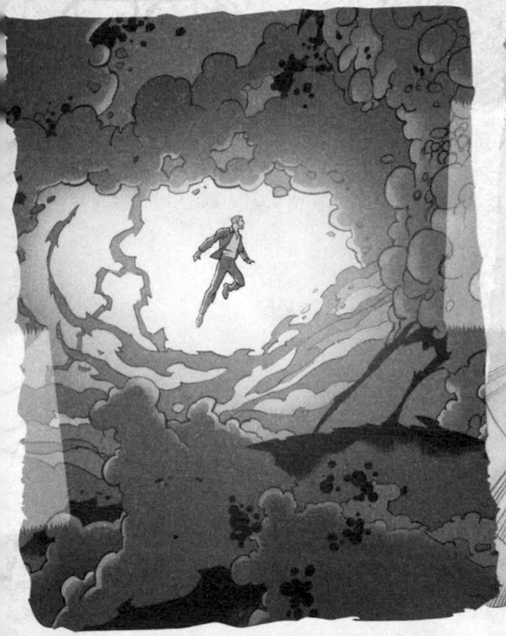

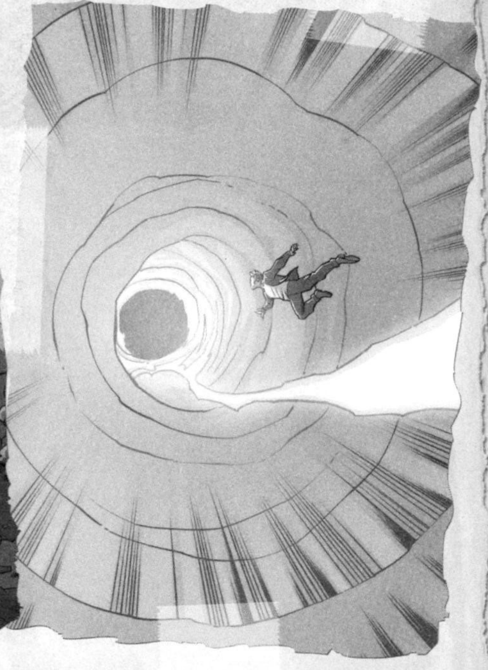

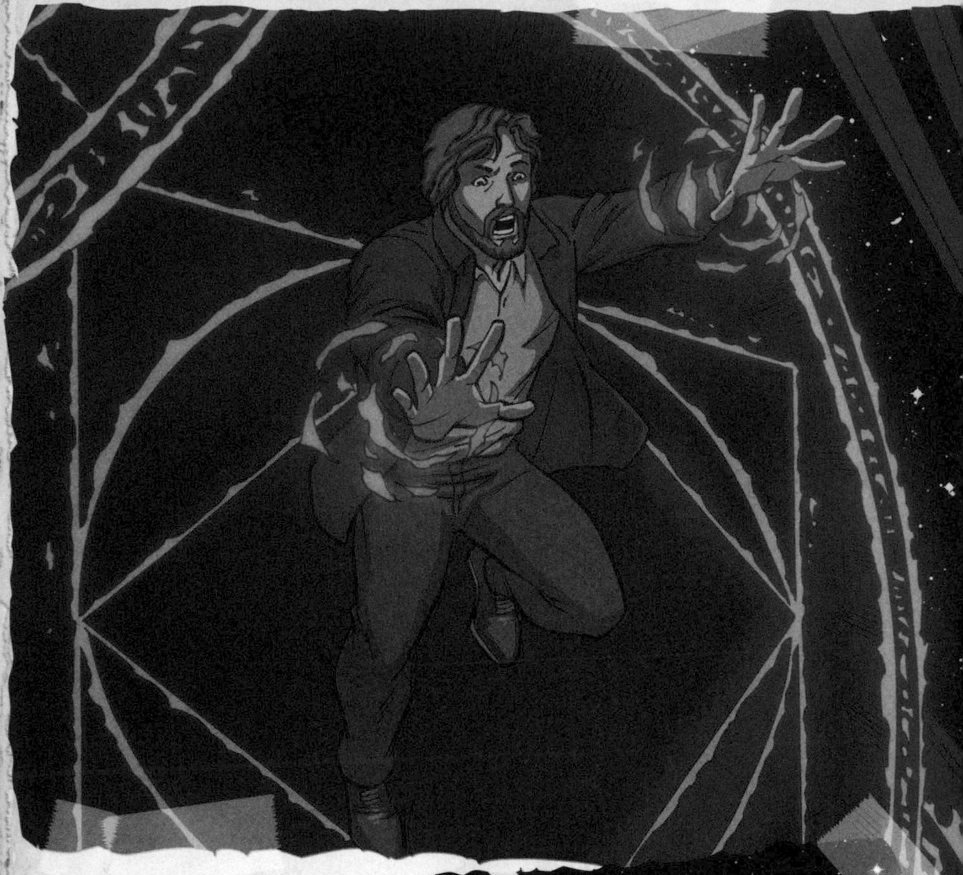

His return to Kamar-Taj and Earth that he knew and recognized wasn't graceful.

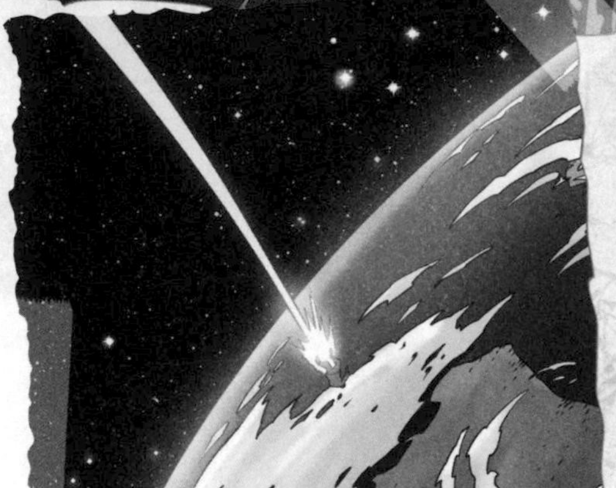

But he came back humbled, and desperate to learn everything that The Ancient One and Mordo had shown him. He didn't just want to fix his hands anymore...He wanted to know it **all**.

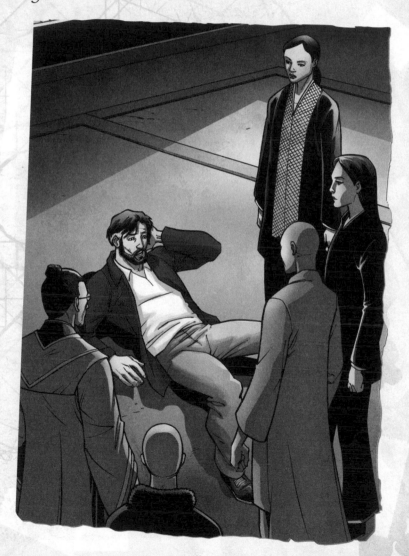

NINE

And so he set out on his months-long training regime. He learned mystic poses and forms, and (sometimes painfully) learned to spar with Mordo.

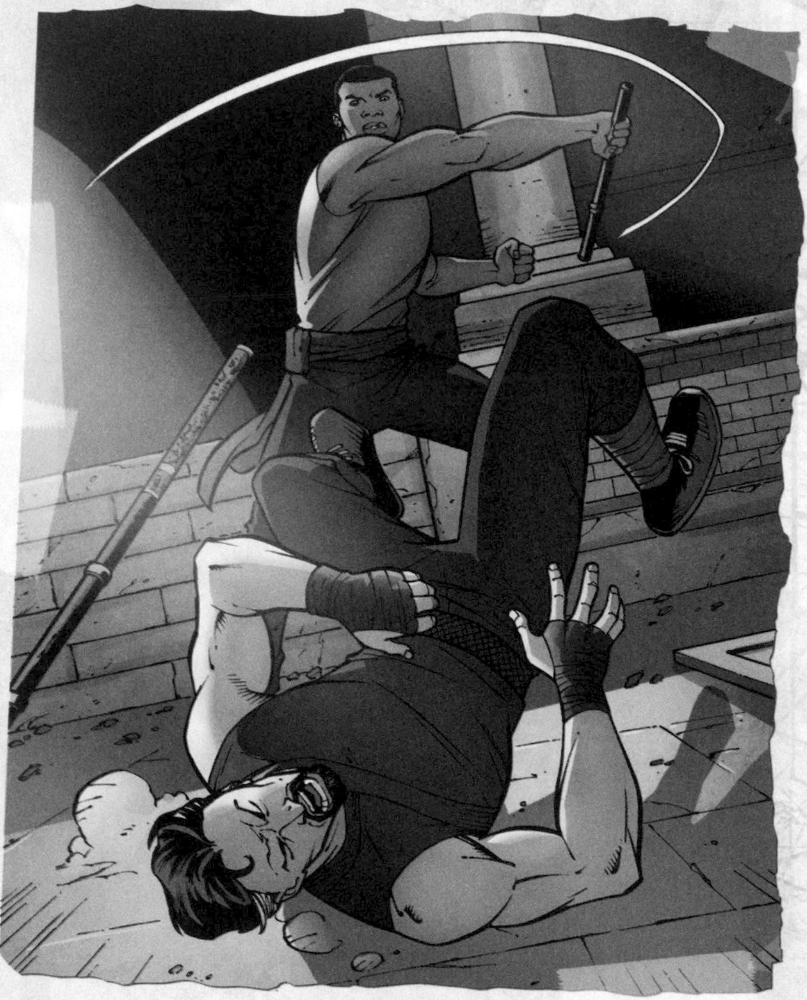

He spent hours in the enormous library, trying to soak up as much knowledge as possible.

And just as he was about to discover something truly remarkable, even in Kamar-Taj terms...

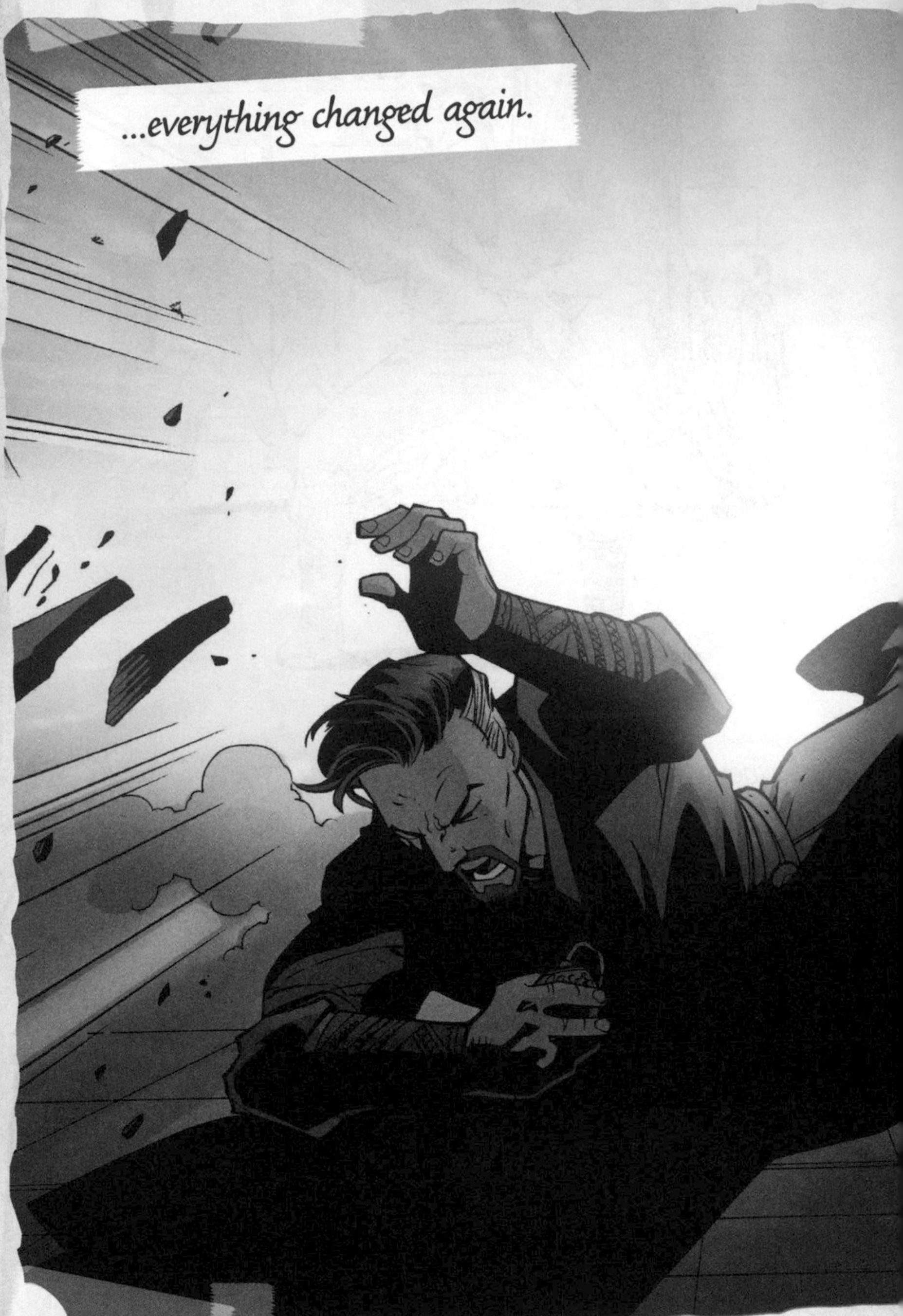
...everything changed again.

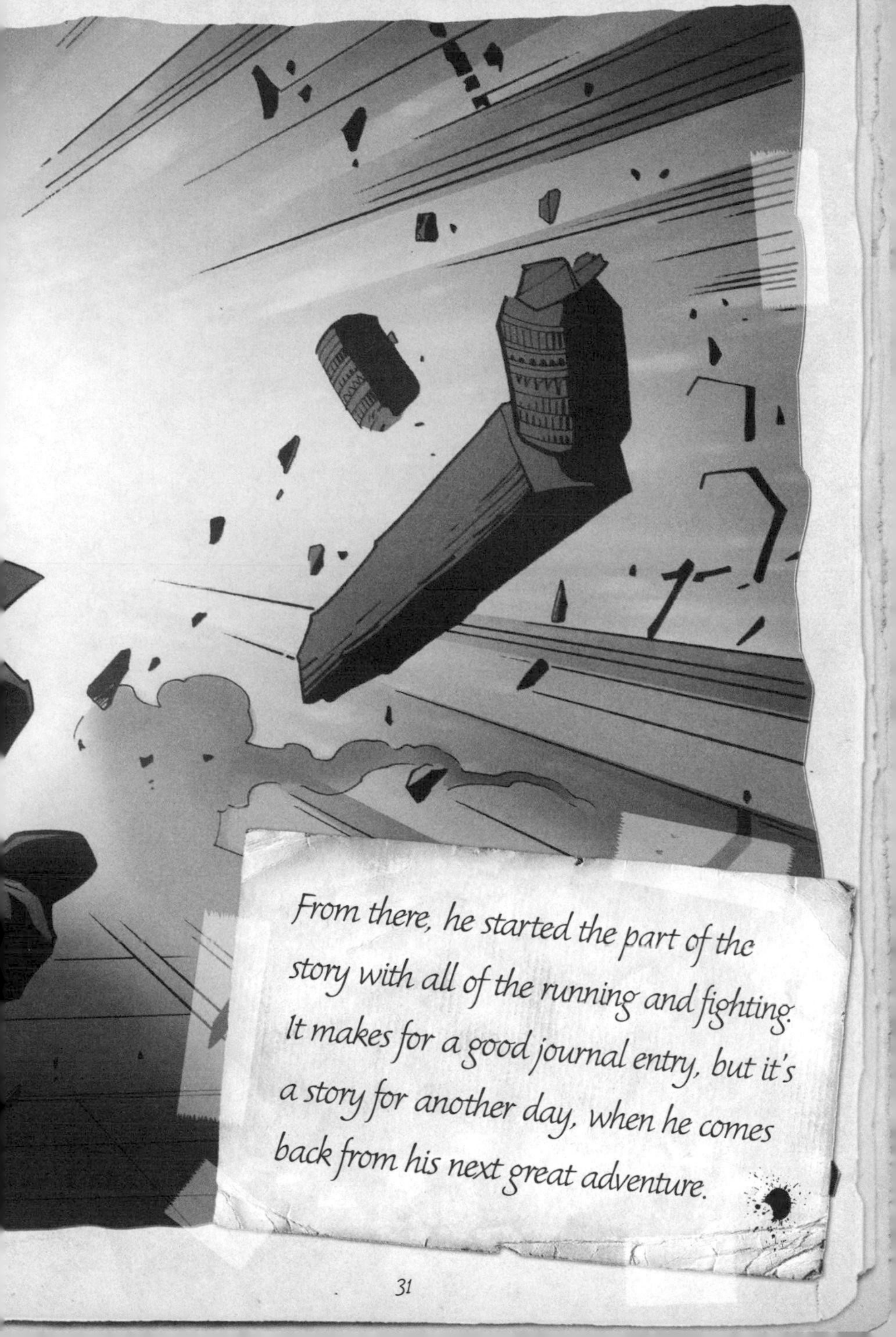

From there, he started the part of the story with all of the running and fighting. It makes for a good journal entry, but it's a story for another day, when he comes back from his next great adventure.

Introduction to the Mystic Arts

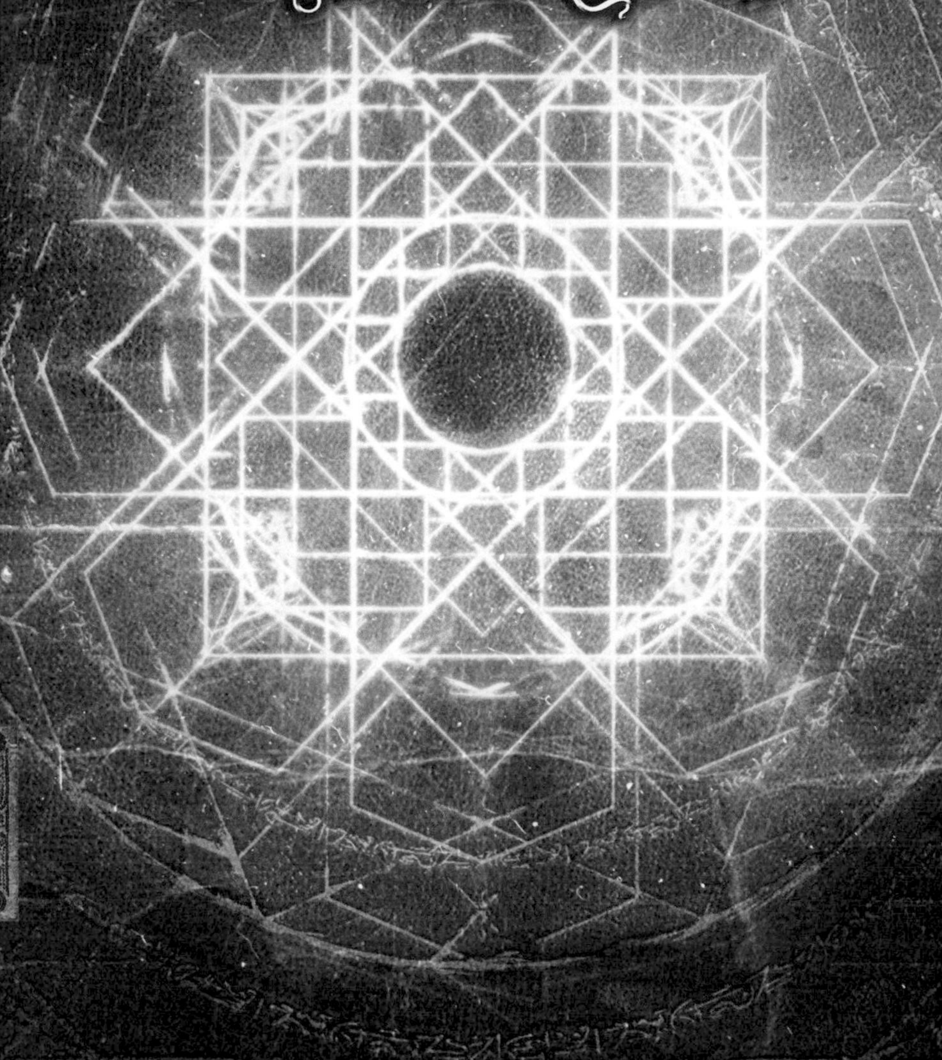

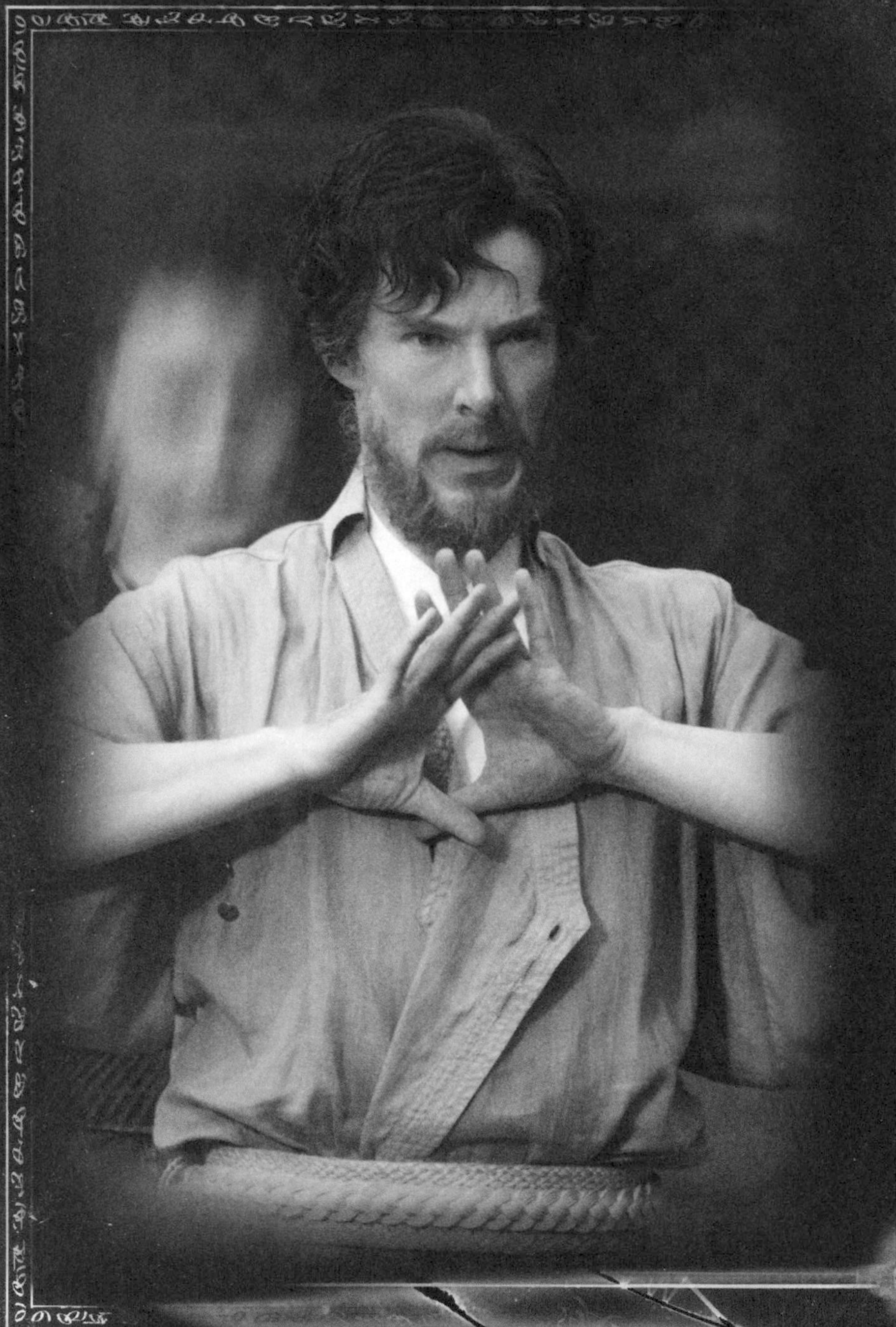

NOTE:

This is an accounting of the knowledge acquired by Doctor Stephen Strange since arriving at Kamar-Taj. The notes may be incomplete in places, but make for a reliable, quick guide. Where available, pictures have been provided for reference.

Kamar-Taj

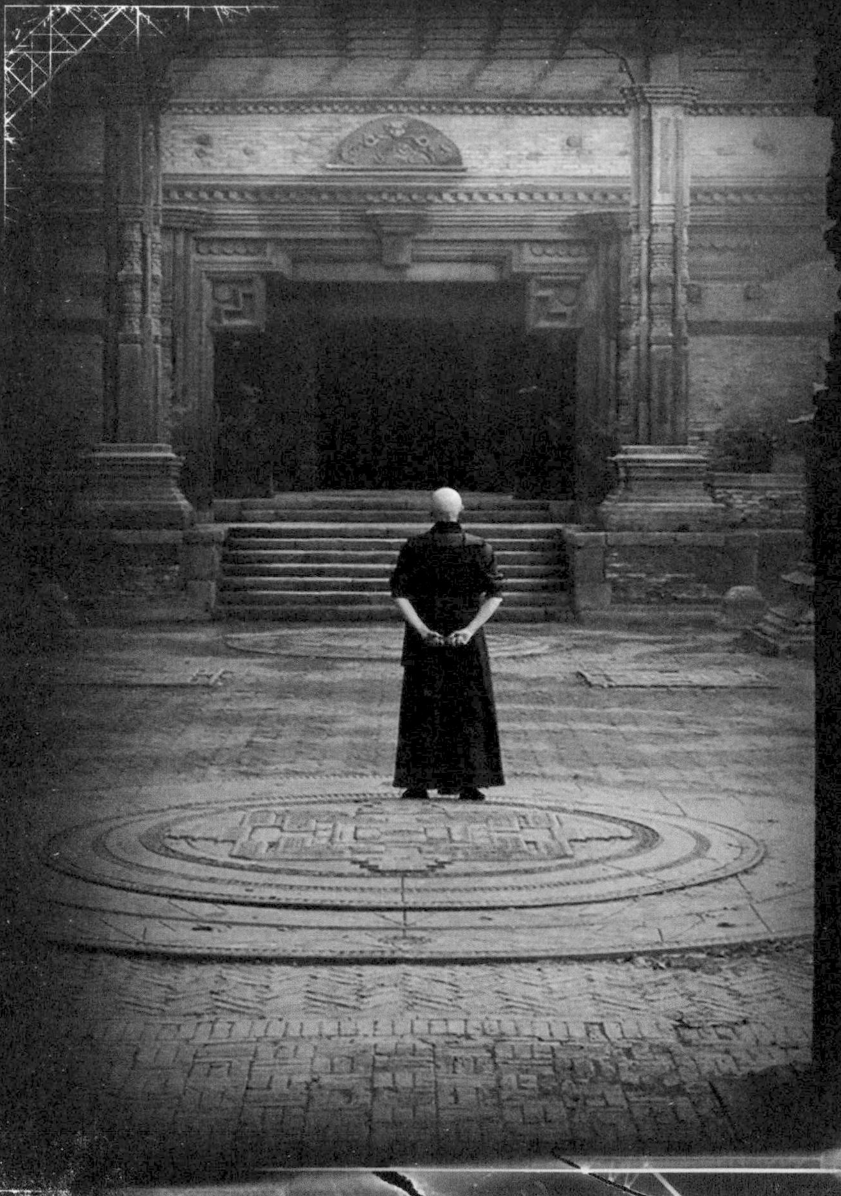

Hidden away in Kathmandu, Kamar-Taj is a unique blend of the mystical and highly modern. Led by The Ancient One and her disciples, travelers from all over the world, including me, Doctor Stephen Strange, have come to seek its miraculous knowledge. While not all are successful, for those with the dedication and fortitude, Kamar-Taj is the birthplace of their new lives as sorcerers.

The Ancient One

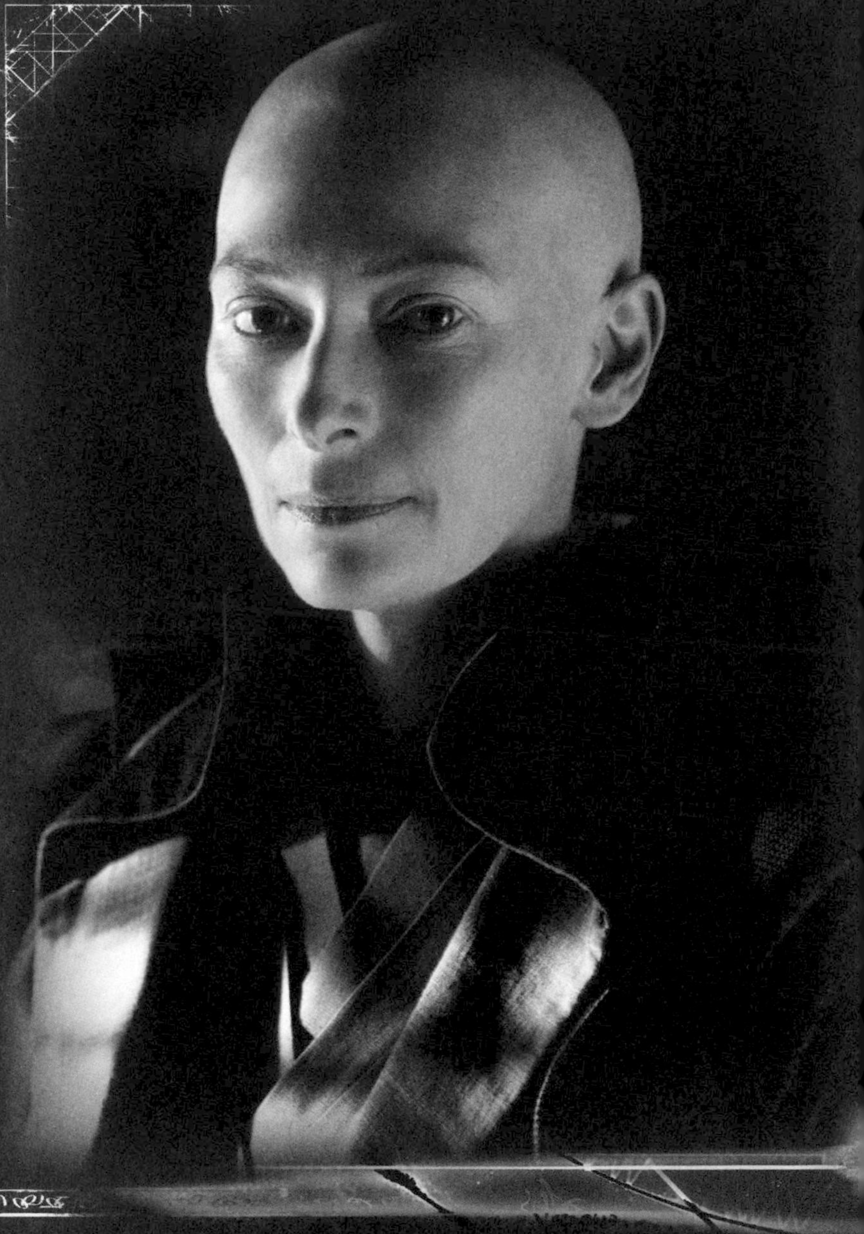

Not much is known about the history of The Ancient One. She is a font of mystical knowledge, and leads the students of Kamar-Taj on their journeys into mystery. She could be impossibly old, or she could just be incredibly experienced in a short time...Either way, she appears beyond formidable in the mystic arts.

Mordo

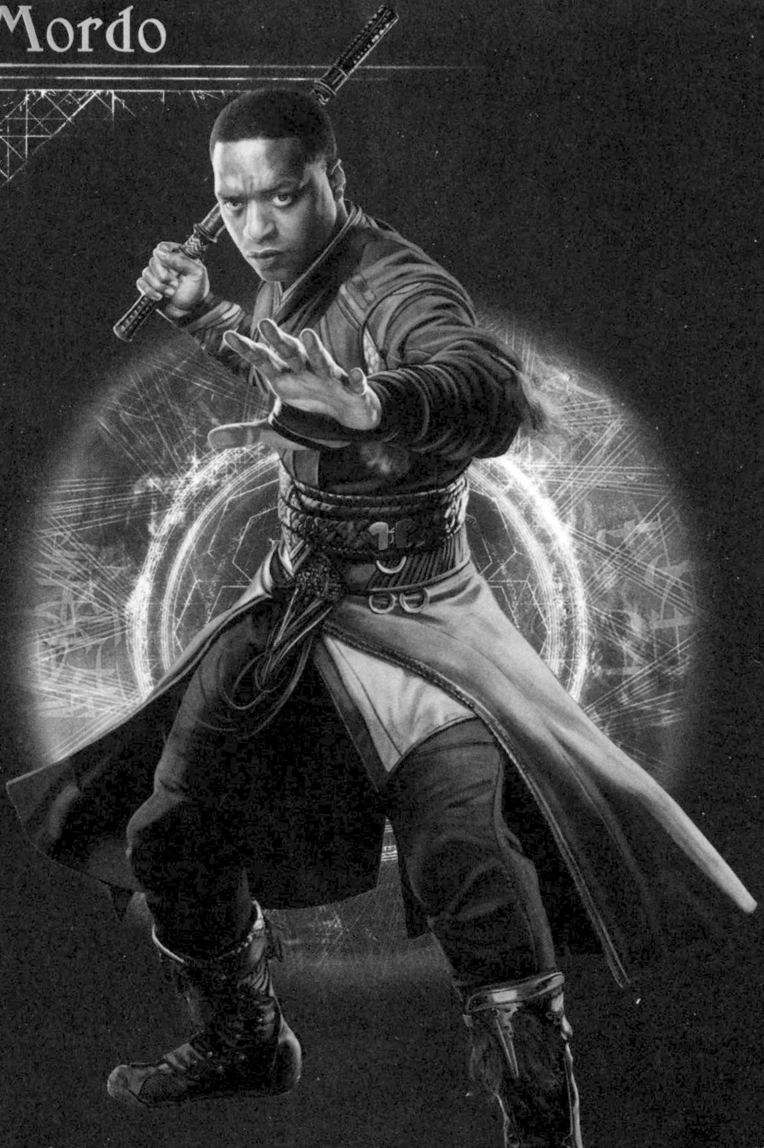

Mordo is an advanced student of The Ancient One, and is responsible for seeking out and selecting new students for training. He wields the Staff of the Living Tribunal and excels in martial arts. He has the advanced knowledge of one who has resided in Kamar-Taj for a long time, but is characteristically tight-lipped about his past.

SEE PAGE 62 FOR REFERENCE

The Narthex

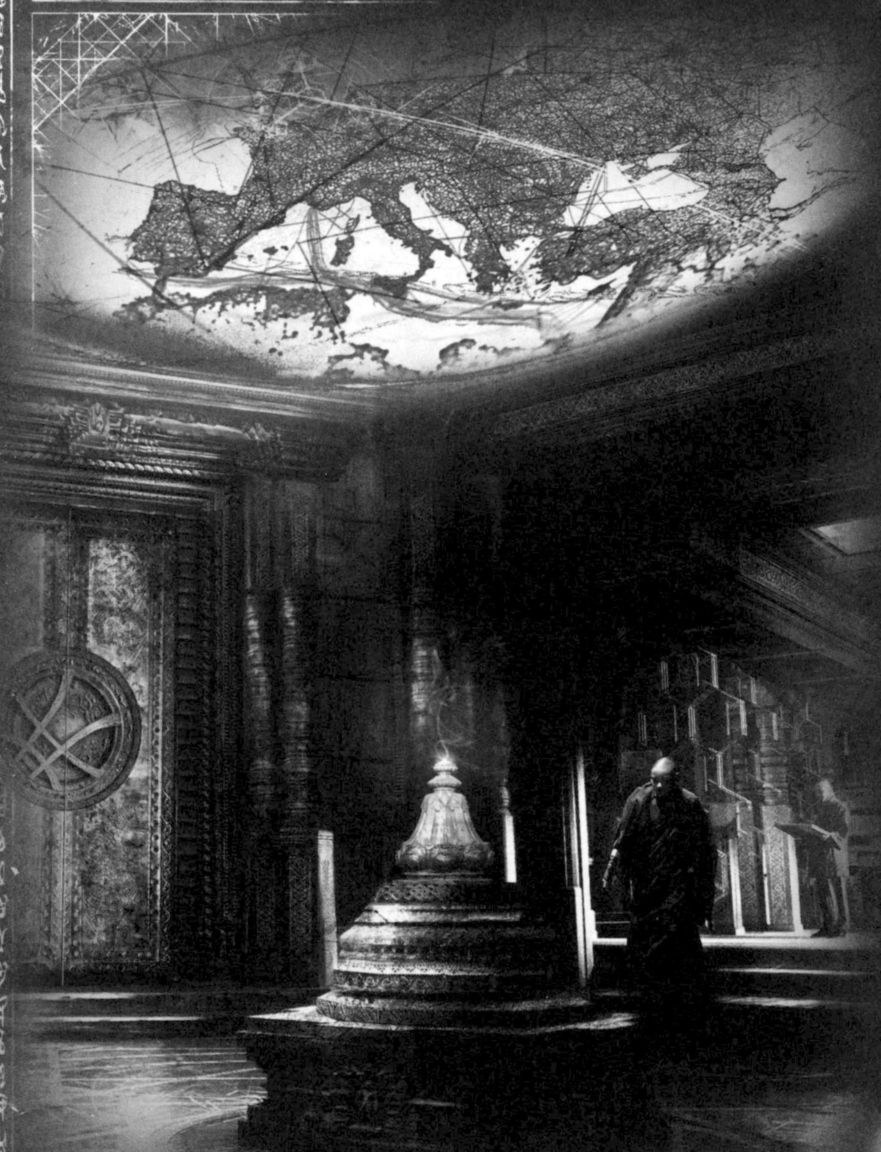

Kamar-Taj is home to worlds of knowledge, so it makes sense that its library would be massively impressive. It's lined with old books, none of which exist outside its walls. Beyond introductory texts, there is a special section curated by the Narthex's librarian/protector, Wong, which is reserved for only Masters.

The Sling Ring

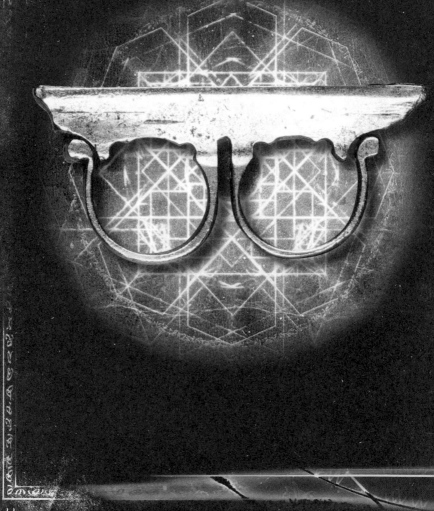

These metal finger ornaments are used as channels that aid the students at Kamar-Taj in accessing their mystical abilities. A sling ring is used to create Earth-bound gateways of sorts. These portals allow the wearer to travel great distances in an instant.

A design on the top—purely speculatively—must help with the connection between sling ring and magical elements it communicates with.

NOTE: ASK WONG THE TRUE SIGNIFICANCE WHEN YOU NEXT SEE HIM.

Each sling ring has two slots for the wearer's fingers, presumably to help secure it physically and spiritually to the wearer.

ALSO, I'VE FOUND THEY LOOK A LITTLE BETTER THIS WAY.

Sling Ring Training

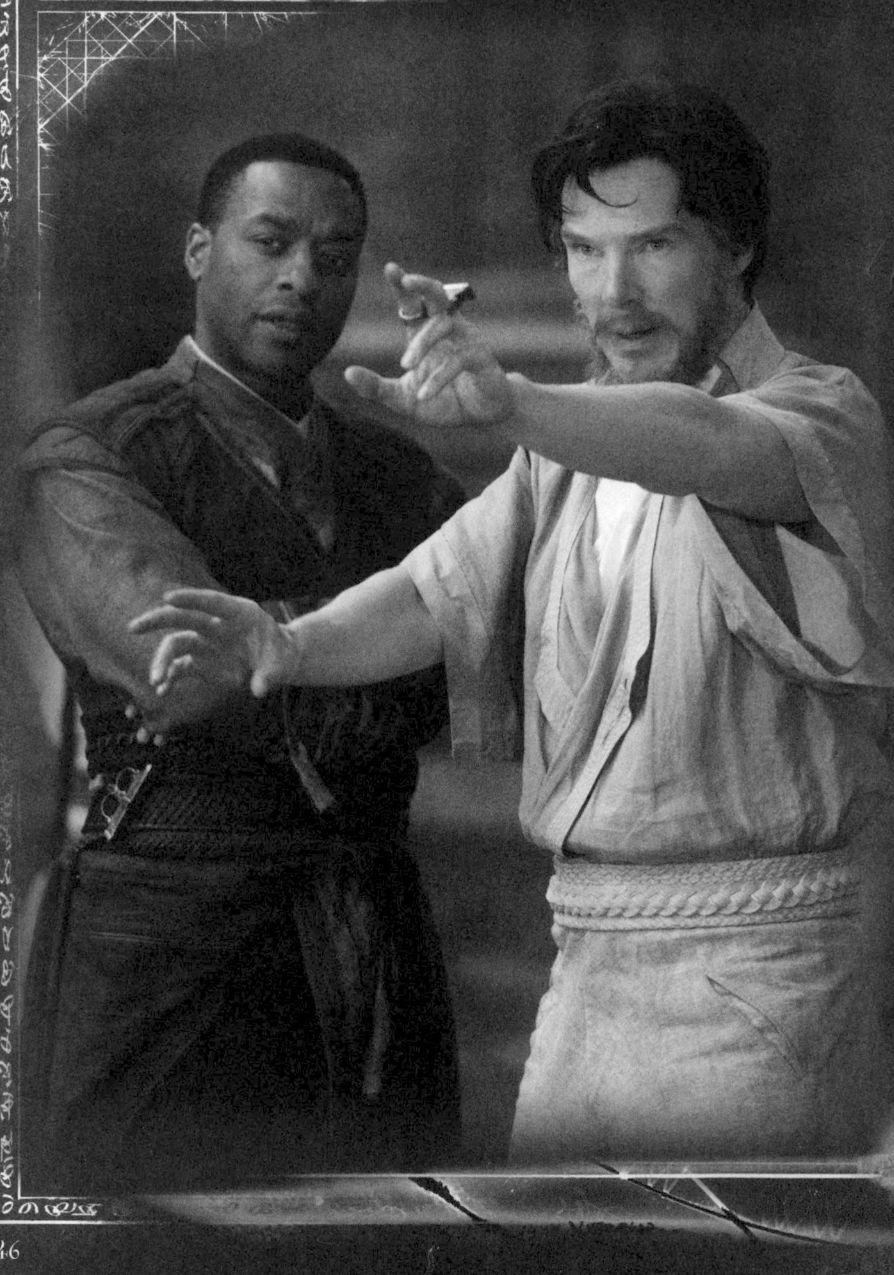

In order to unlock the power of the sling ring, practitioners must master several basic poses. These poses serve to help unlock physical energy from the user, and, combined with meditation and the focus of the sling ring, the sorcerer is then able to tap into greater magical powers. Poses and movements become more complex with more advanced magic.

The Astral Plane

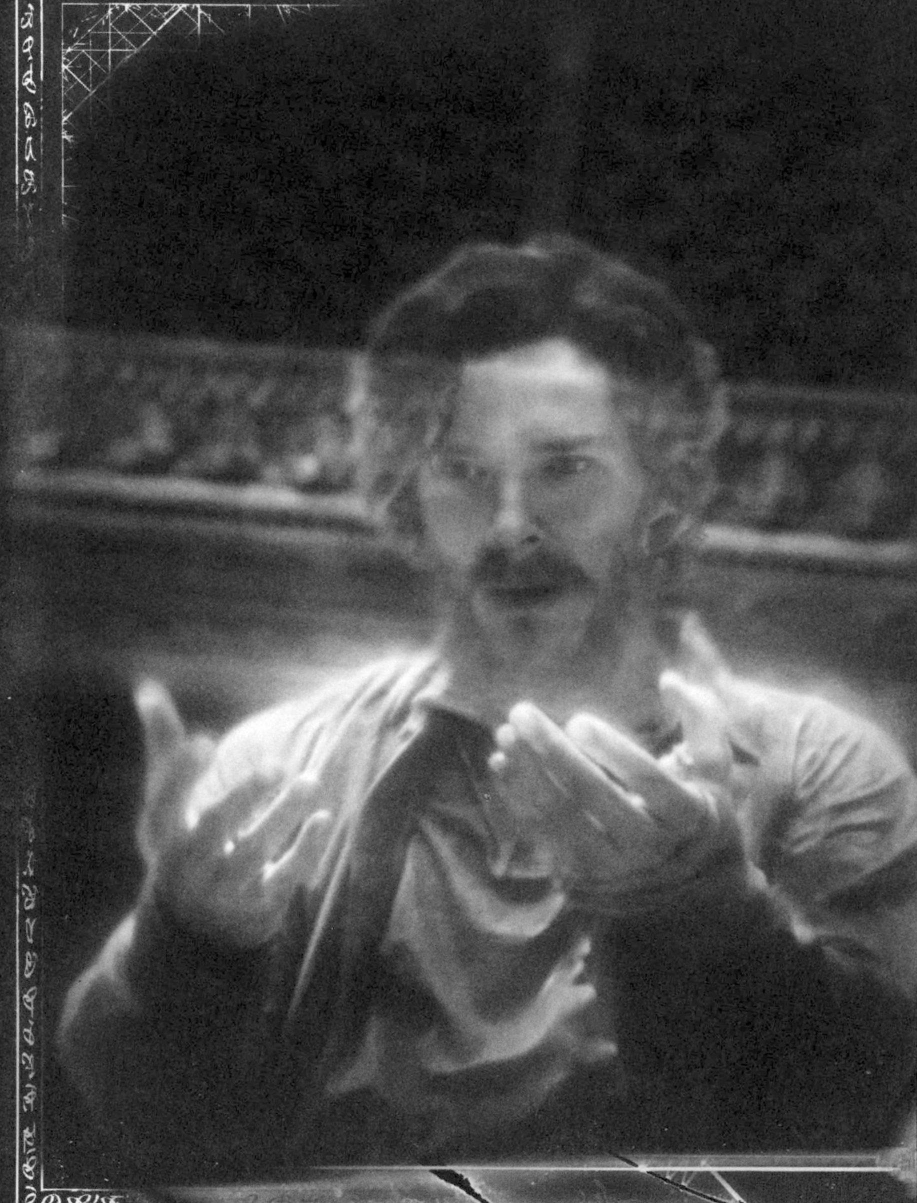

Inside each of us is an astral projection of, for lack of a better word, our spirit. A skilled practitioner can separate this astral form from the physical form, providing a literal out-of-body experience.

THE ANCIENT ONE DEMONSTRATING

Robes of the Novice

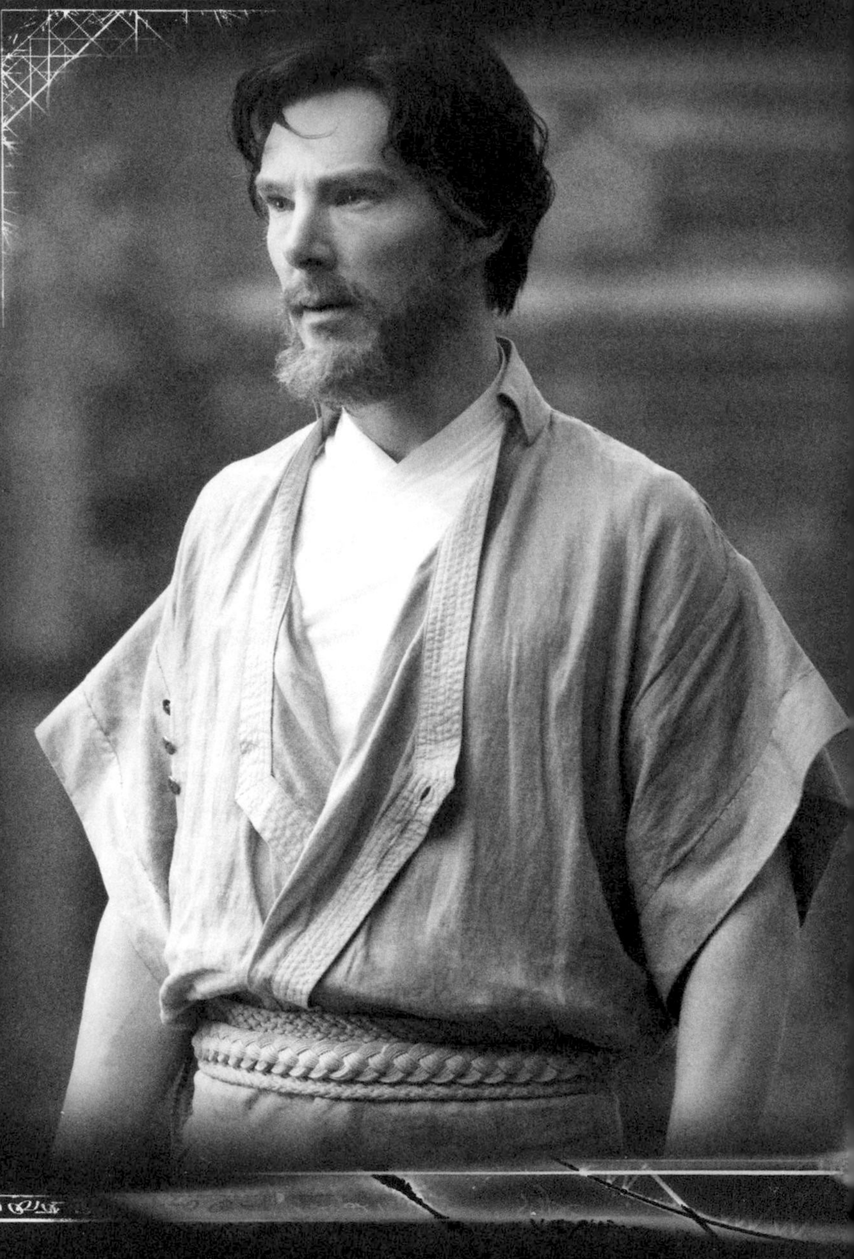

Every mystic begins their journey in the robes of a novice.

Each set of robes signifies to both the wearer and the teacher the acolyte's current level of mastery over the mystical arts taught in Kamar-Taj.

This simple gray uniform is made for the most basic practitioner, with each subsequent level symbolically rewarded with a new set of clothes.

Robes of the Master

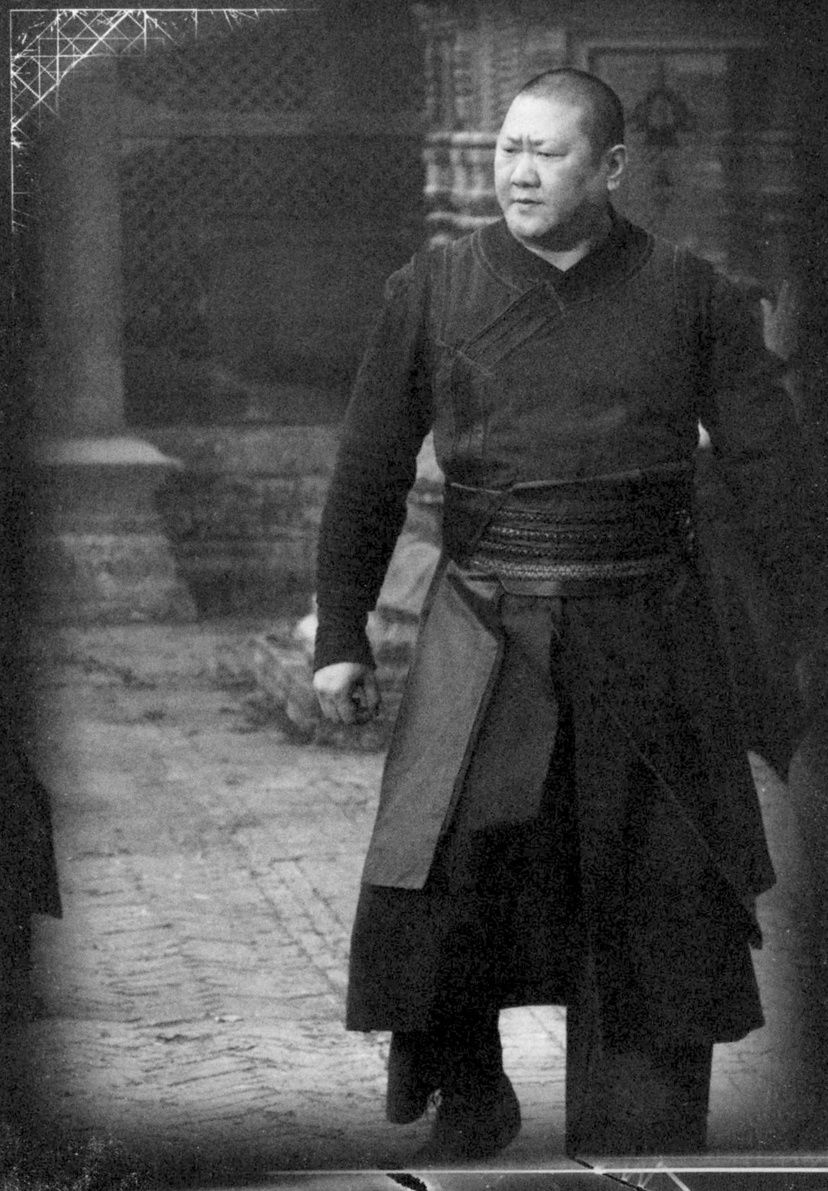

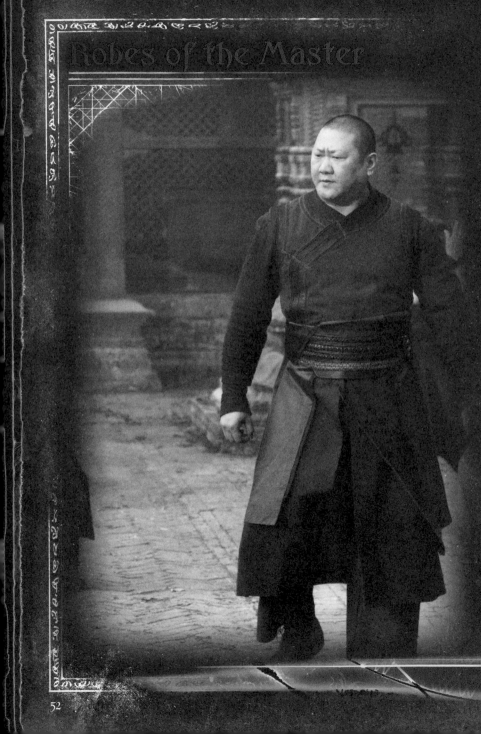

Modeled here by the caretaker and guardian of the Narthex, Wong, the robes of the Master are darker in color, and are a symbol of years of learning and training. At this moment, the extent of a Master's power has not been made clear, but if Wong is any indicator, these robes signify an enormous knowledge of the mystic arts.

Mandalas and Symbols

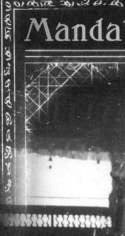

The Ancient One teaches that there is great power in certain symbols. Each is complicated and unique, and with practice a sorcerer can summon any number of useful energy projections, defenses, and portals to other locations.

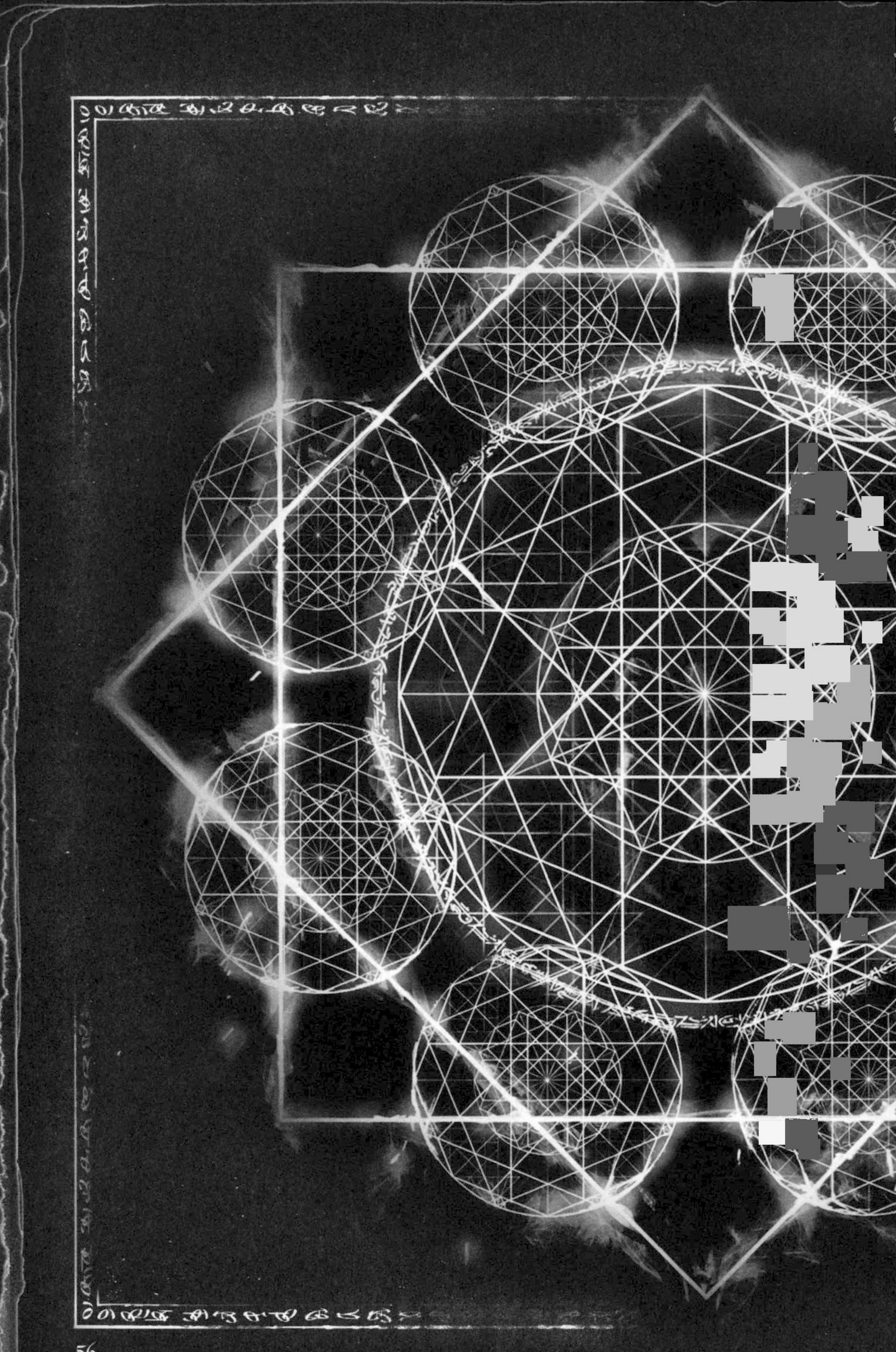

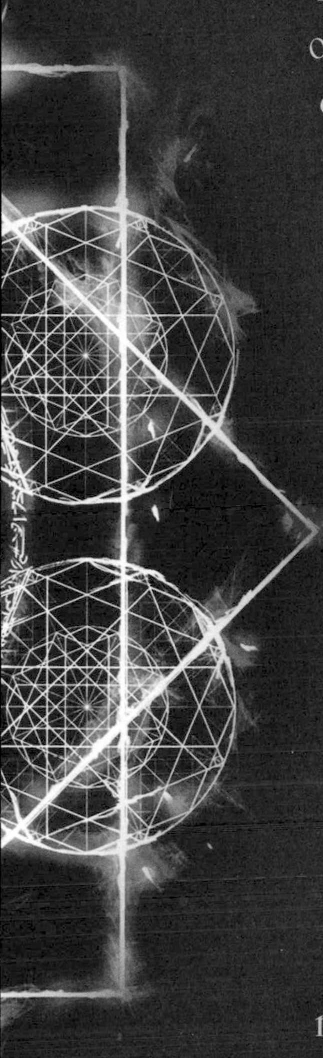

While these symbols are ornate and beautiful, each one takes careful attention to detail to master, and even more to discover. The Ancient One speaks of them as though each is a letter in a larger word, building on one another for greater strength and meaning.

That said, they remain largely mysterious to most novices.

The Sanctum Sanctorum

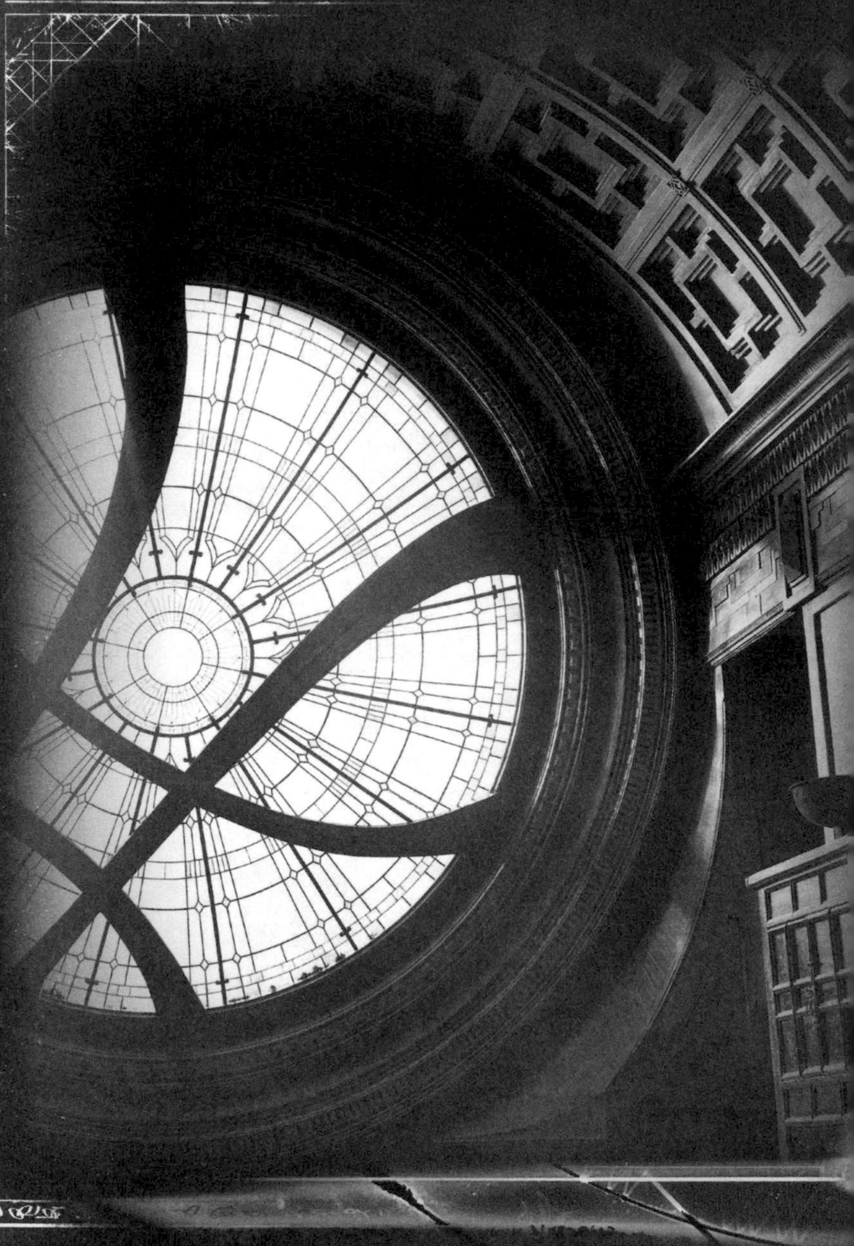

Around the world are three Sanctum Sanctorums. They exist where key lines of mystic power intersect, and serve as houses of sanctuary and holding for a wide array of relics. Each Sanctum is monitored closely in Kamar-Taj, and acts as an early warning system for certain types of planetary and dimensional threats.

Interestingly enough, one Sanctum Sanctorum is in Greenwich Village, New York City, disguised in plain sight as a quaint brownstone.

Each Sanctum features a rotunda, with ever-changing portals to other parts of the world, enabling quick travel to anywhere a sorcerer might need to go.

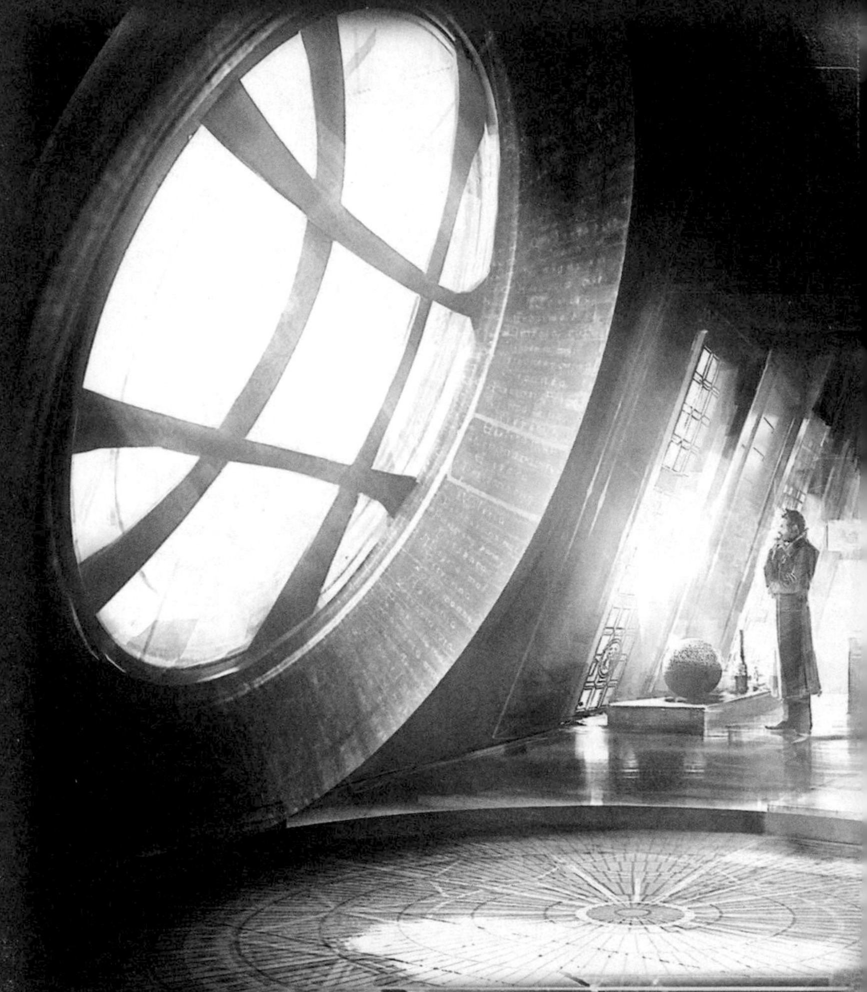

One defining characteristic of the Sanctums is the unique window pattern. While definitely important, its true meaning is still obscured.

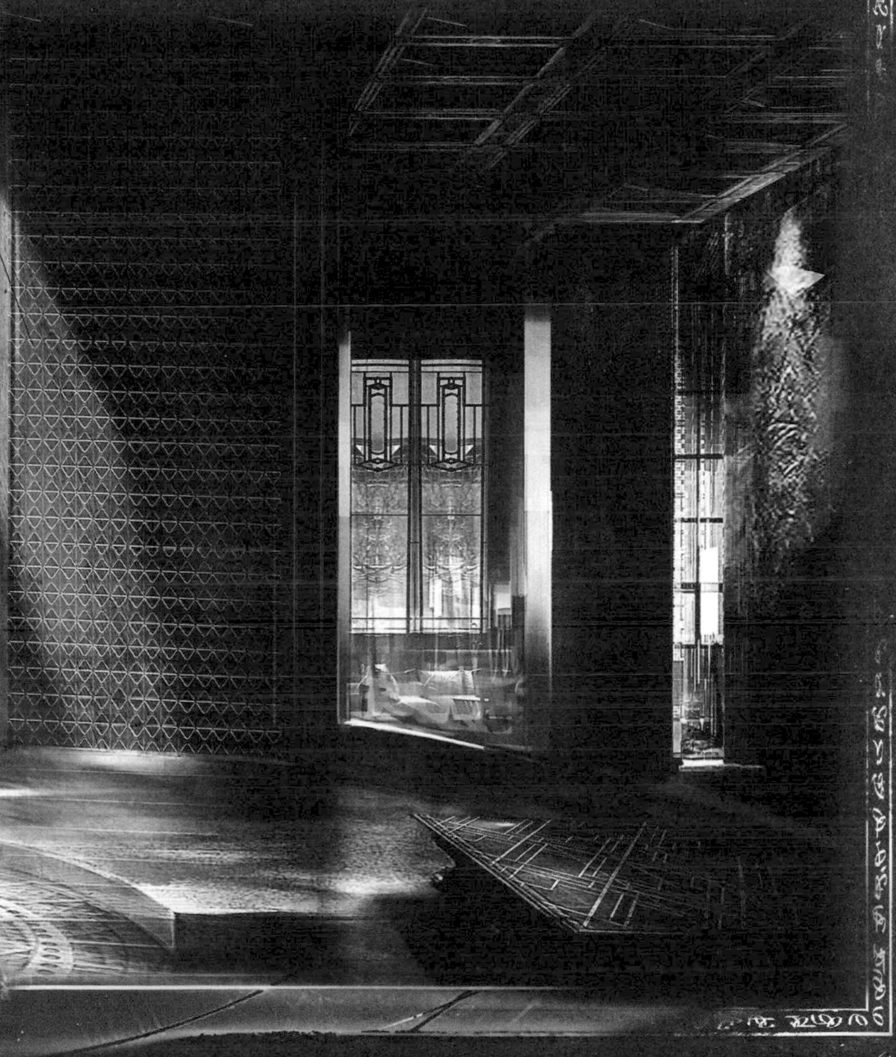

The Staff of the Living Tribunal

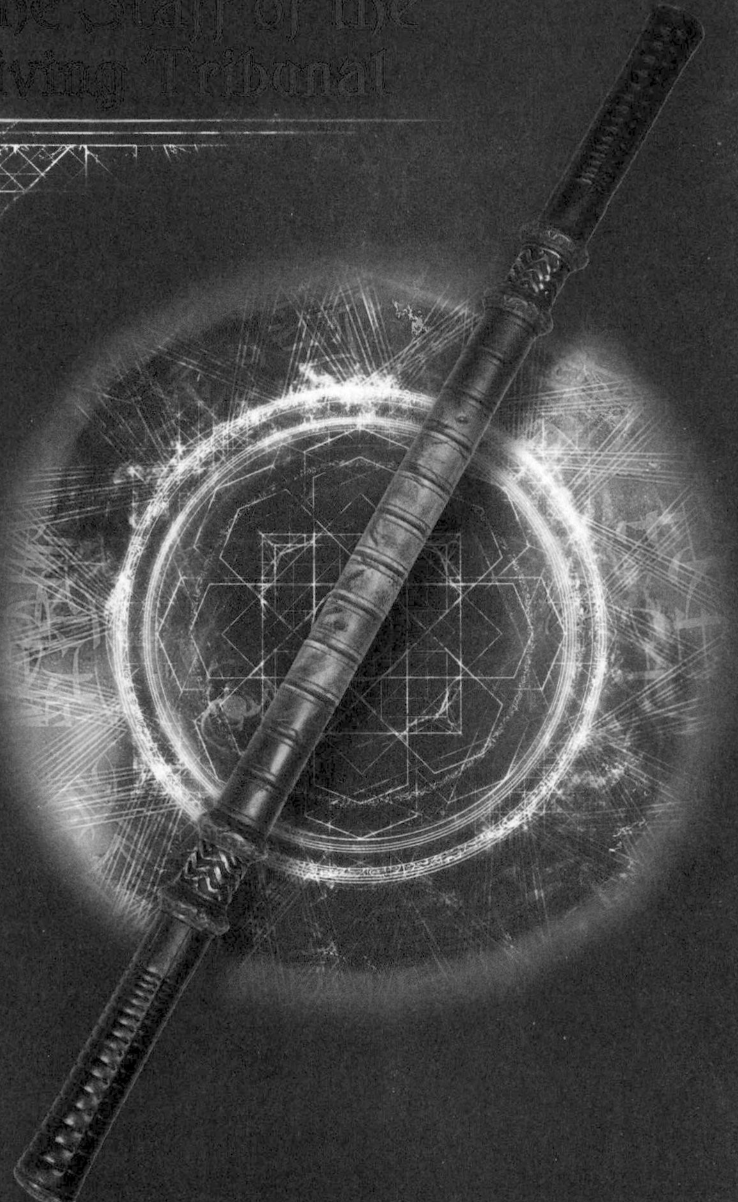

Ancient relics like the Staff of the Living Tribunal are exceptionally rare.

Certain spells require more strength than can be consistently applied by one practitioner—so items like this staff are imbued with those magical energies instead, providing a reliable (and safer) source of power.

The Living Tribunal, after whom this staff is named, is a being of cosmic importance and, from what we can understand, near-limitless power.

While the staff itself cannot possibly come close to the same levels of energy as its namesake, by tapping into a greater source of power, it does pack a meaningful punch, well beyond that of a normal weapon's.

The Cloak of Levitation

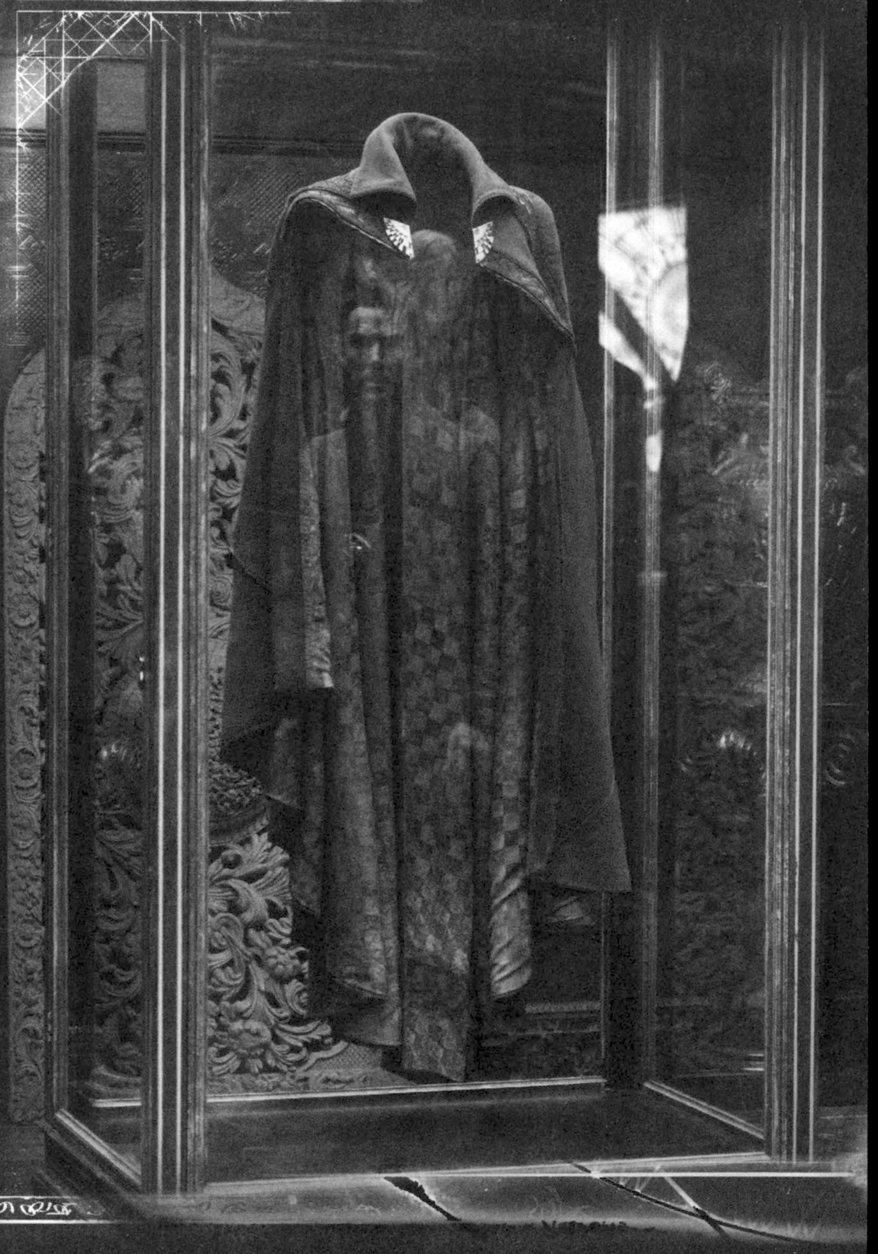

Another relic, this cloak is housed in the Sanctum Sanctorum in New York City.

Its origins are largely unknown, but it does appear to take on a life of its own from time to time. The wearer is granted the ability of limited flight (hence the name Cloak of Levitation) and it appears to have defensive capabilities.

NOTE:
THE CLOAK IS SURPRISINGLY STYLISH FOR AN ANCIENT RELIC.

The Eye of Agamotto

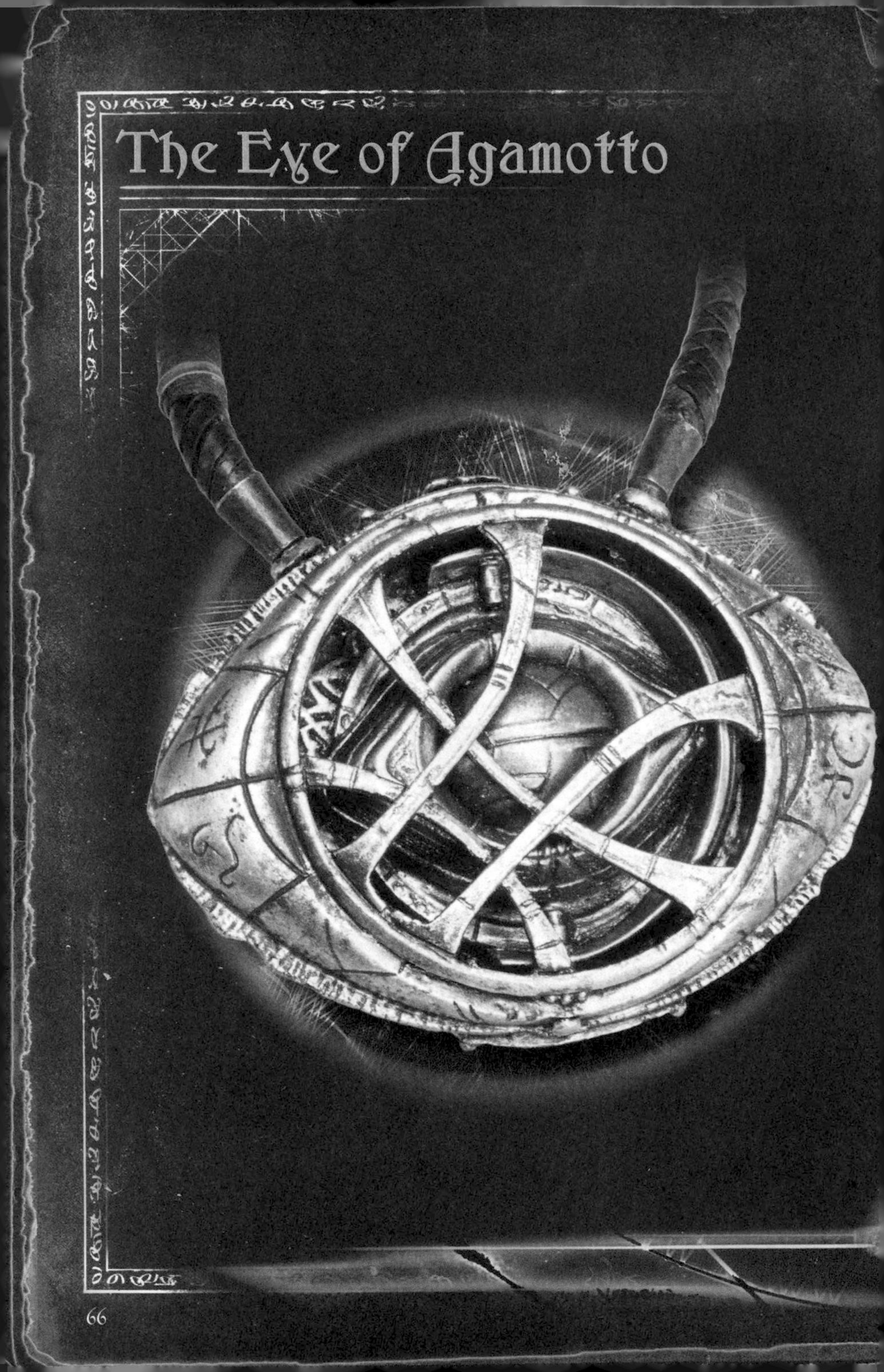

This medallion can be found in the Narthex, although most information about it resides in Wong's restricted section for Masters. It holds a very special place in the library, and appears to change its appearance based on its own perception of situations and people present. Judging by its special placement and the lack of readily available information about it, this is a very important and powerful amulet.

NOTE:
TWO OF THE
APPEARANCES THE
EYE HAS ASSUMED.

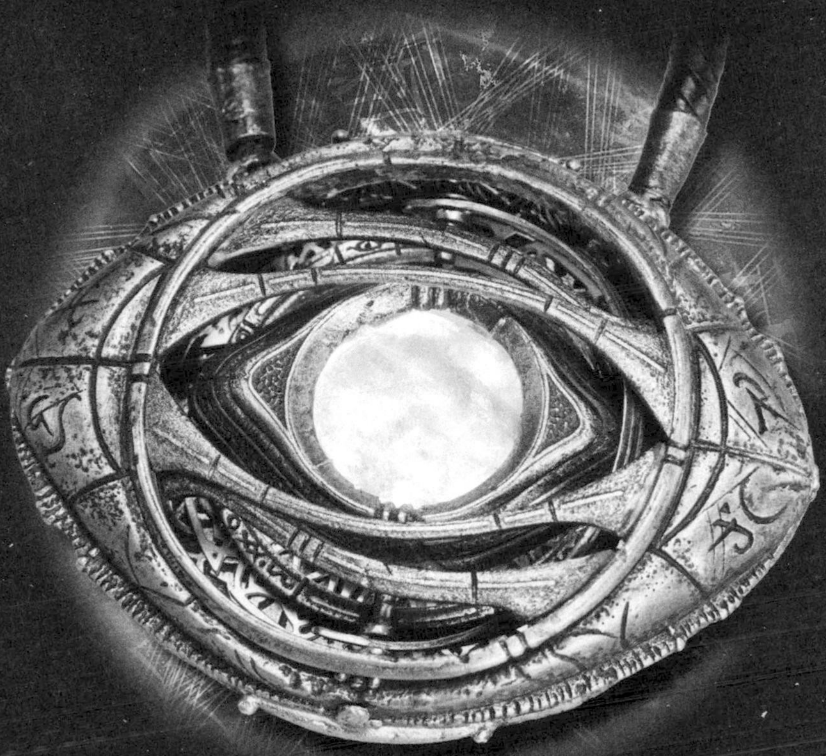

Markings of Kaecilius

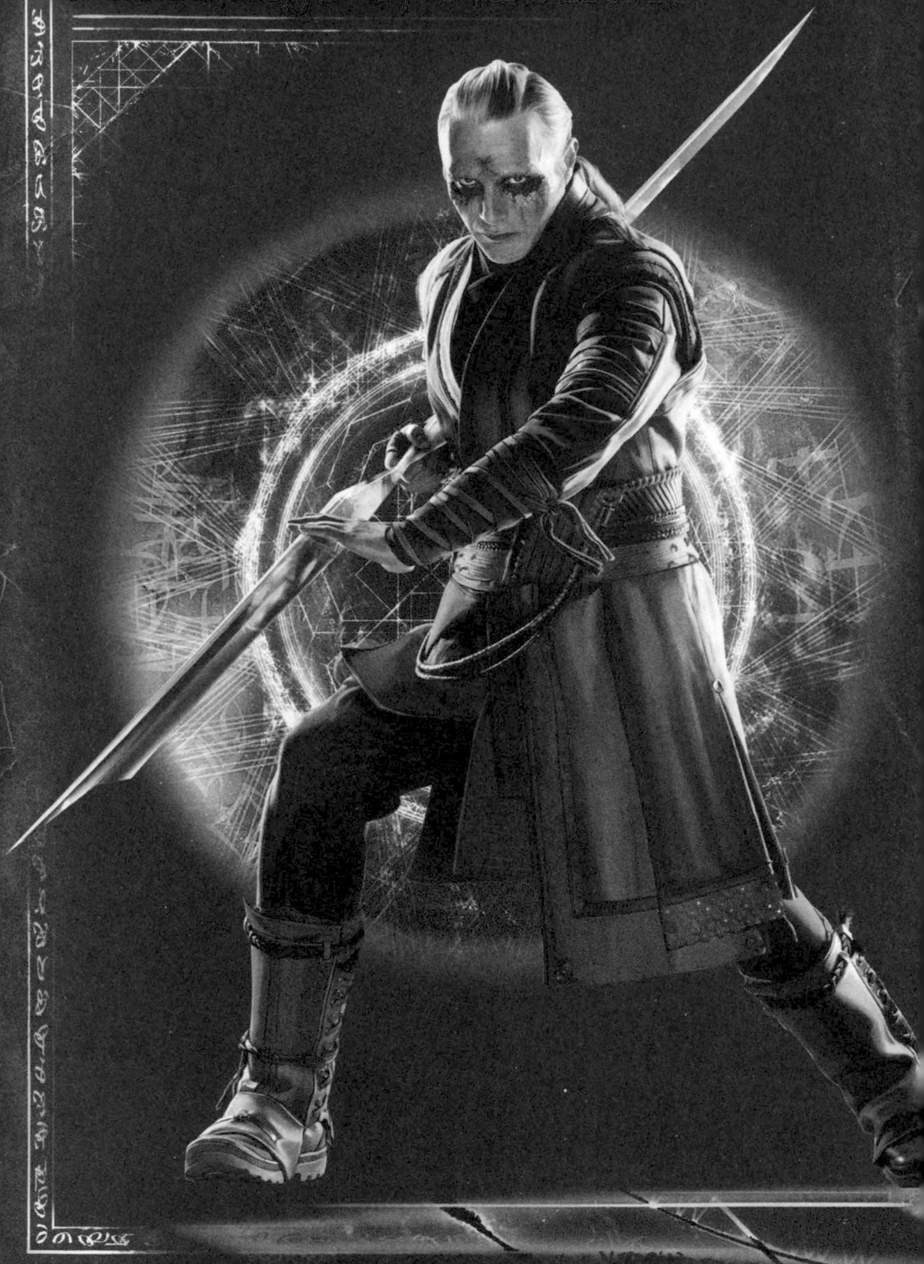

Kaecilius leads the Zealots who broke away from The Ancient One's teachings in search of more power. The dark marks around Kaecilius's eyes are relatively new developments, with precious little information available about what could have caused them or what they mean.

The Zealots

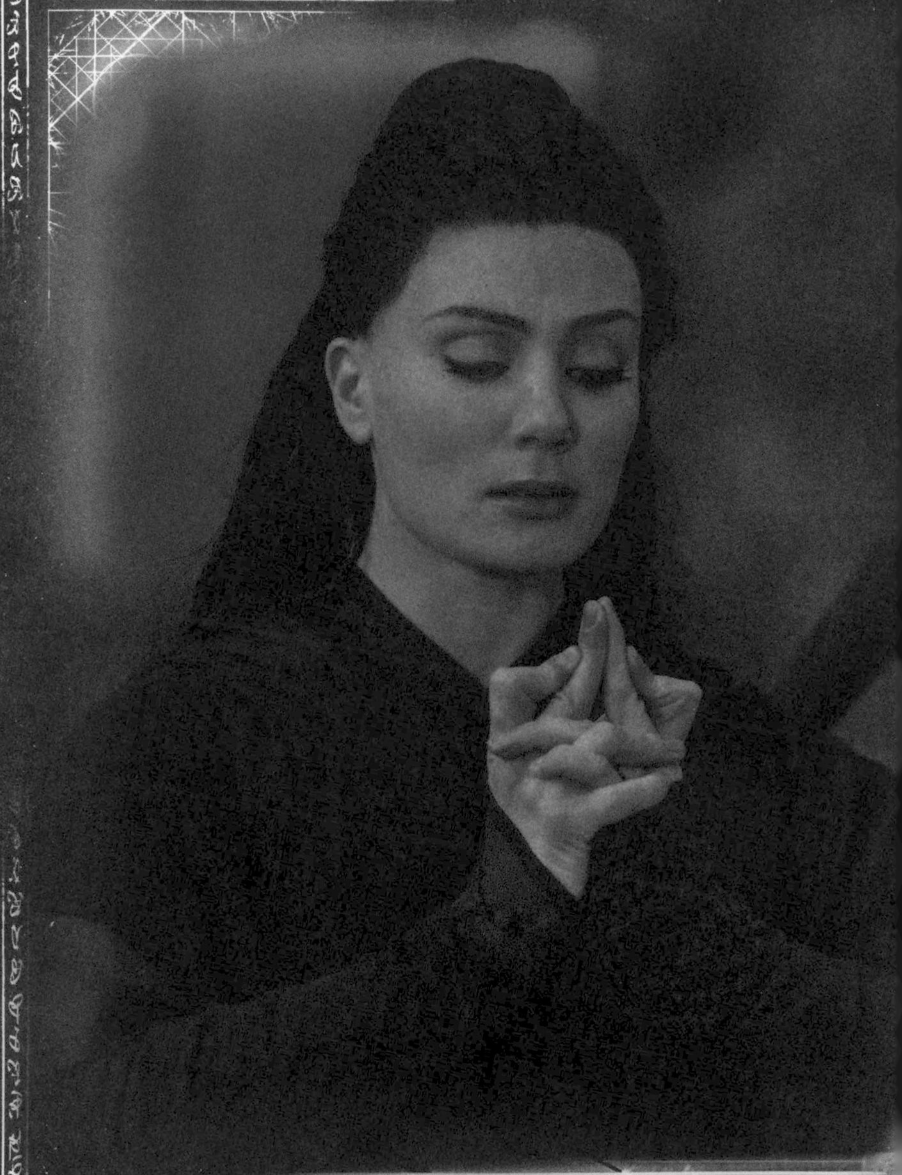

The Zealots following Kaecilius are in search of a greater power that The Ancient One would not teach them. It is rumored that they are looking for a way to artificially extend their lives, but their true intentions are unknown. Records of their movements and whereabouts are painfully incomplete.

Relics and Books for Further Study

NOTE TO SELF:
WHEN TIME ALLOWS, RESEARCH THE FOLLOWING RELICS. DOUBTLESS THEY'LL BE USEFUL AT SOME POINT IN THE FUTURE, BUT WITHOUT COMBING THROUGH THE NARTHEX, THEY REMAIN A BIT OF A MYSTERY.

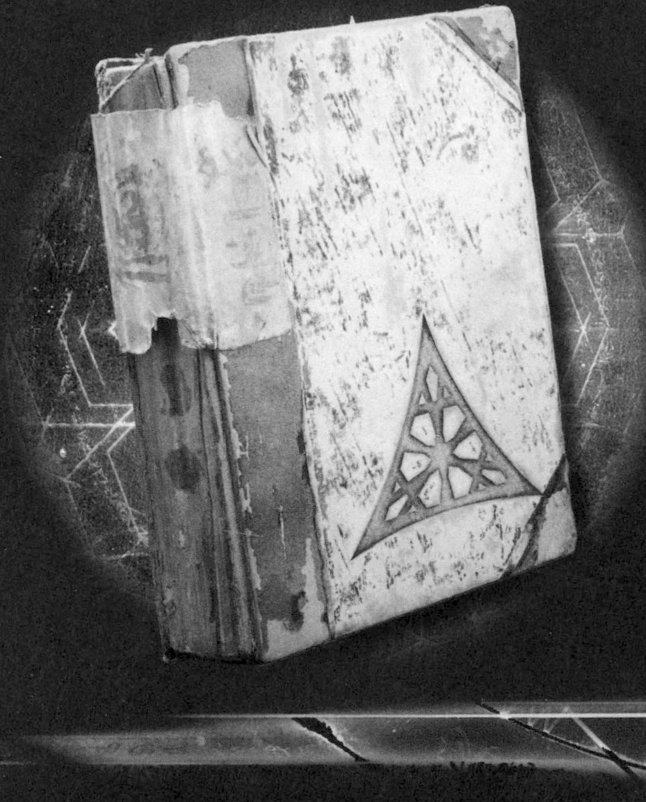

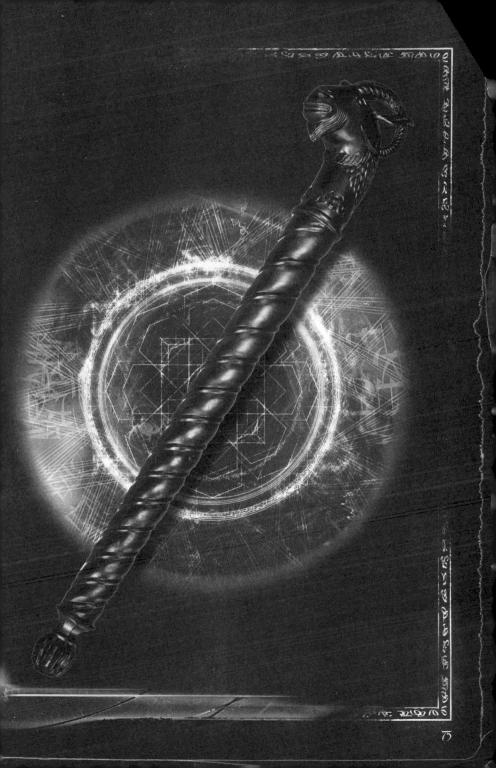

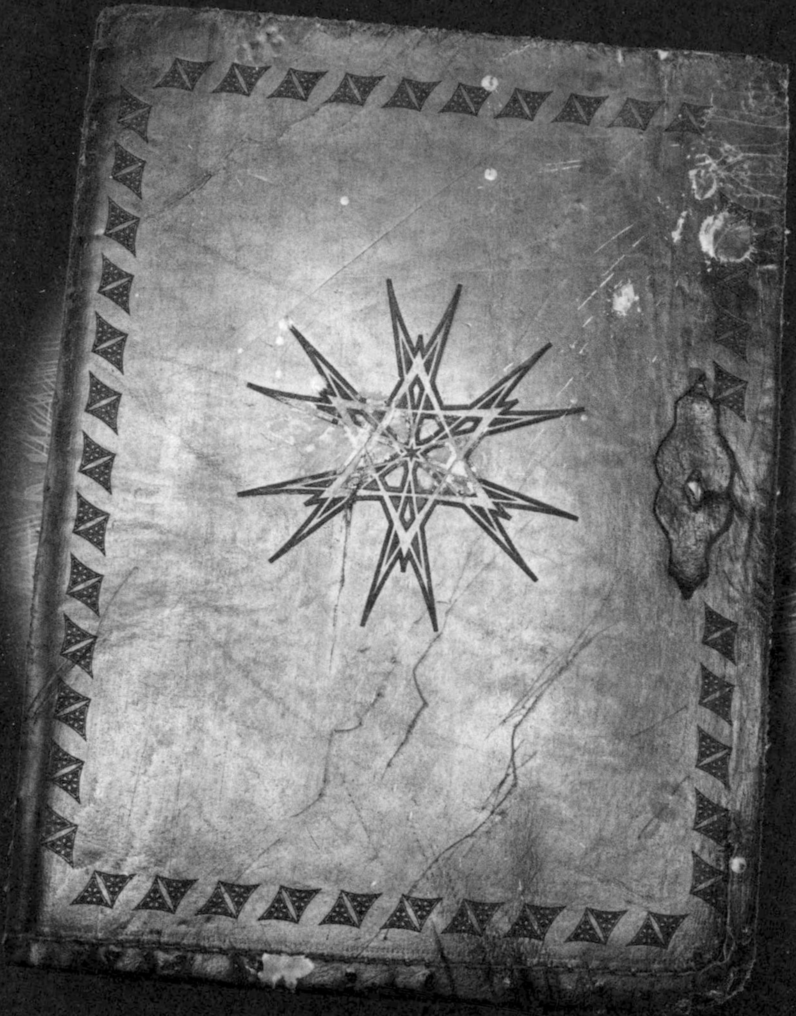

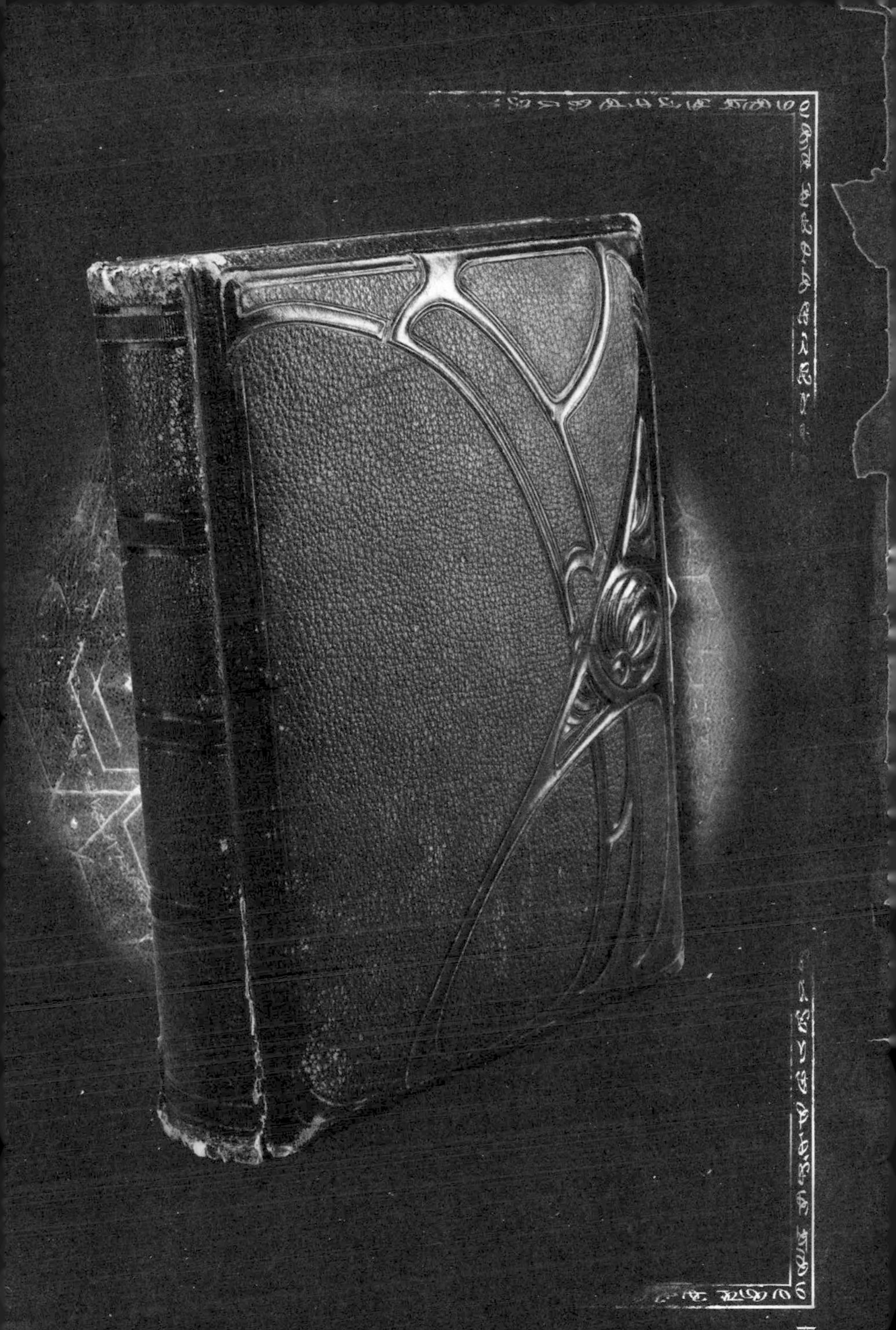

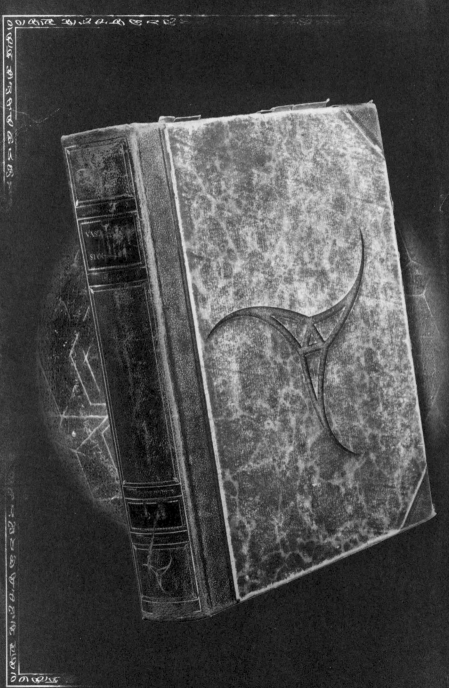

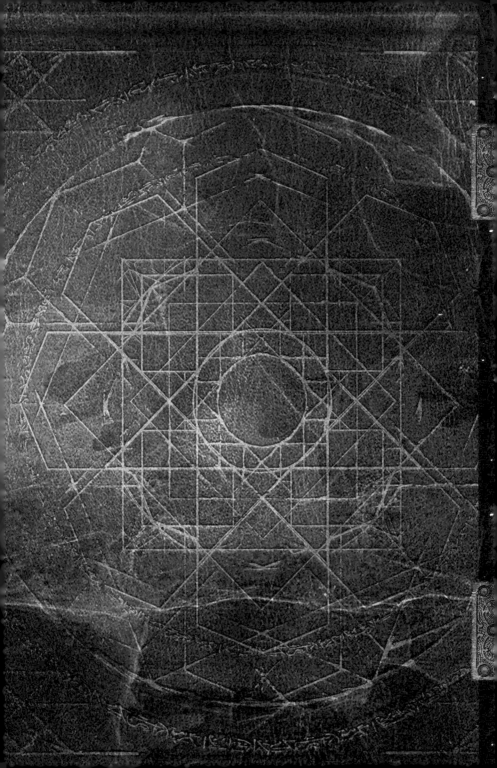

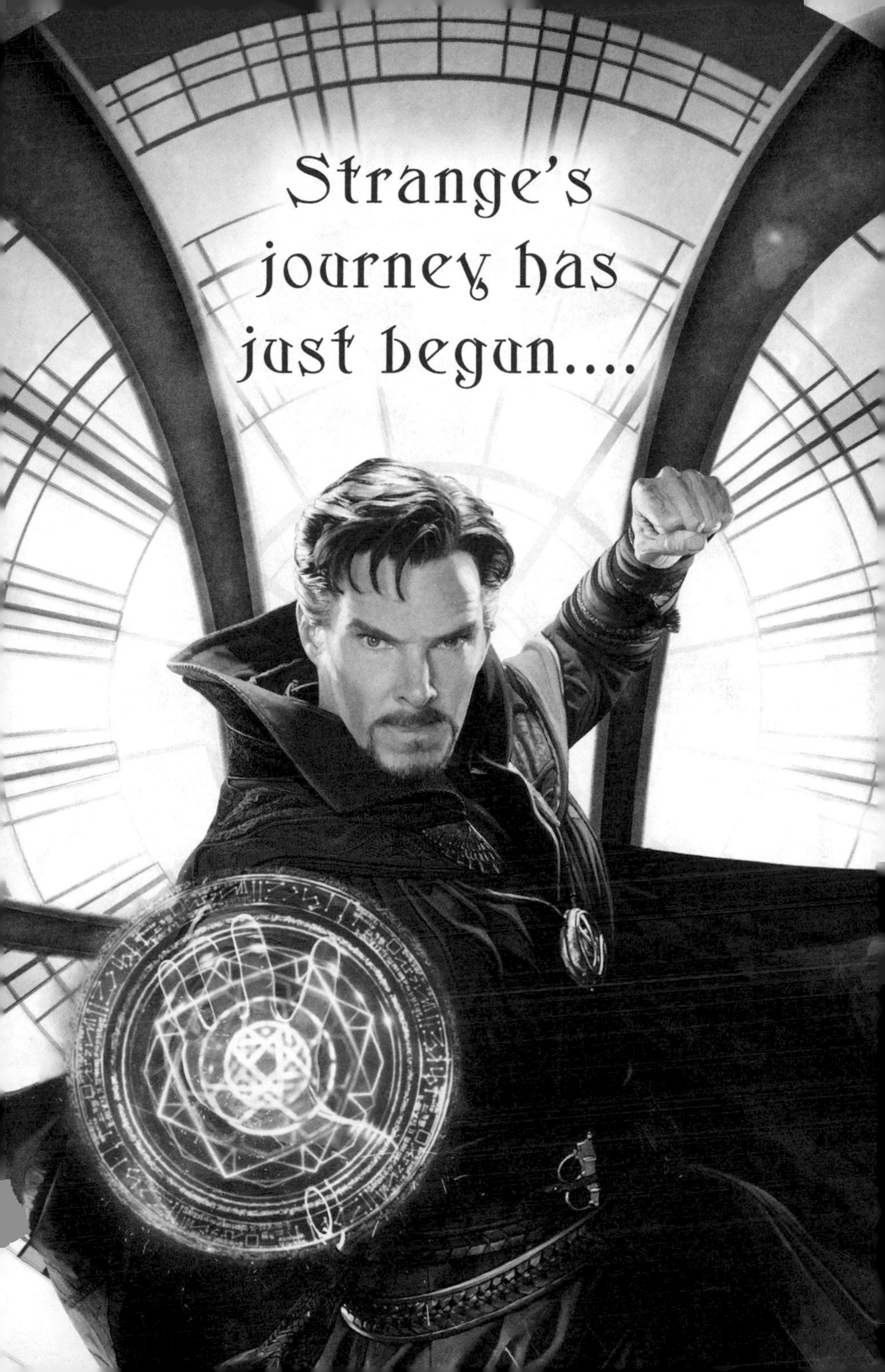
Strange's journey has just begun....

Don't miss...

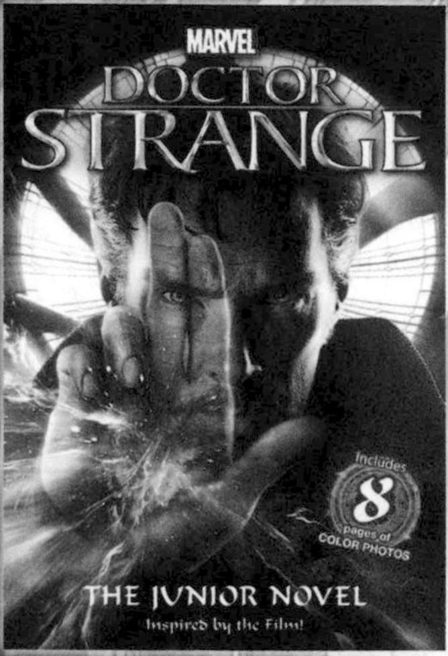
MARVEL
DOCTOR STRANGE
Includes 8 pages of COLOR PHOTOS
THE JUNIOR NOVEL
Inspired by the Film!

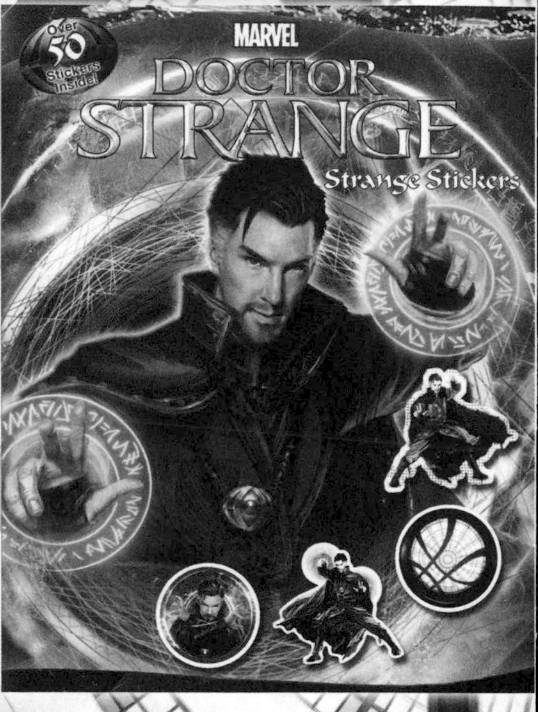
Over 50 Stickers Inside!
MARVEL
DOCTOR STRANGE
Strange Stickers

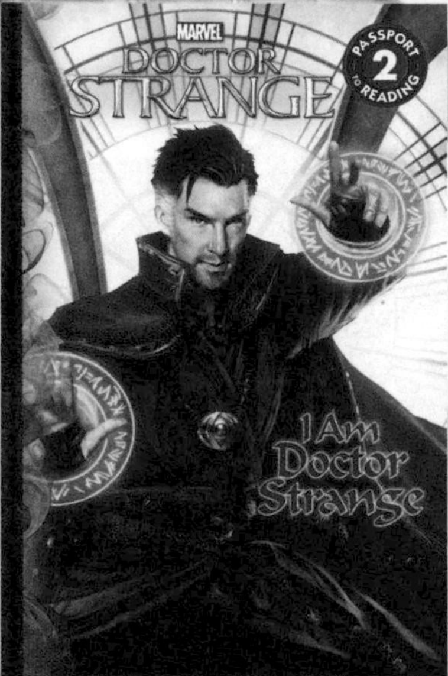
MARVEL
DOCTOR STRANGE
PASSPORT 2 TO READING
I Am Doctor Strange

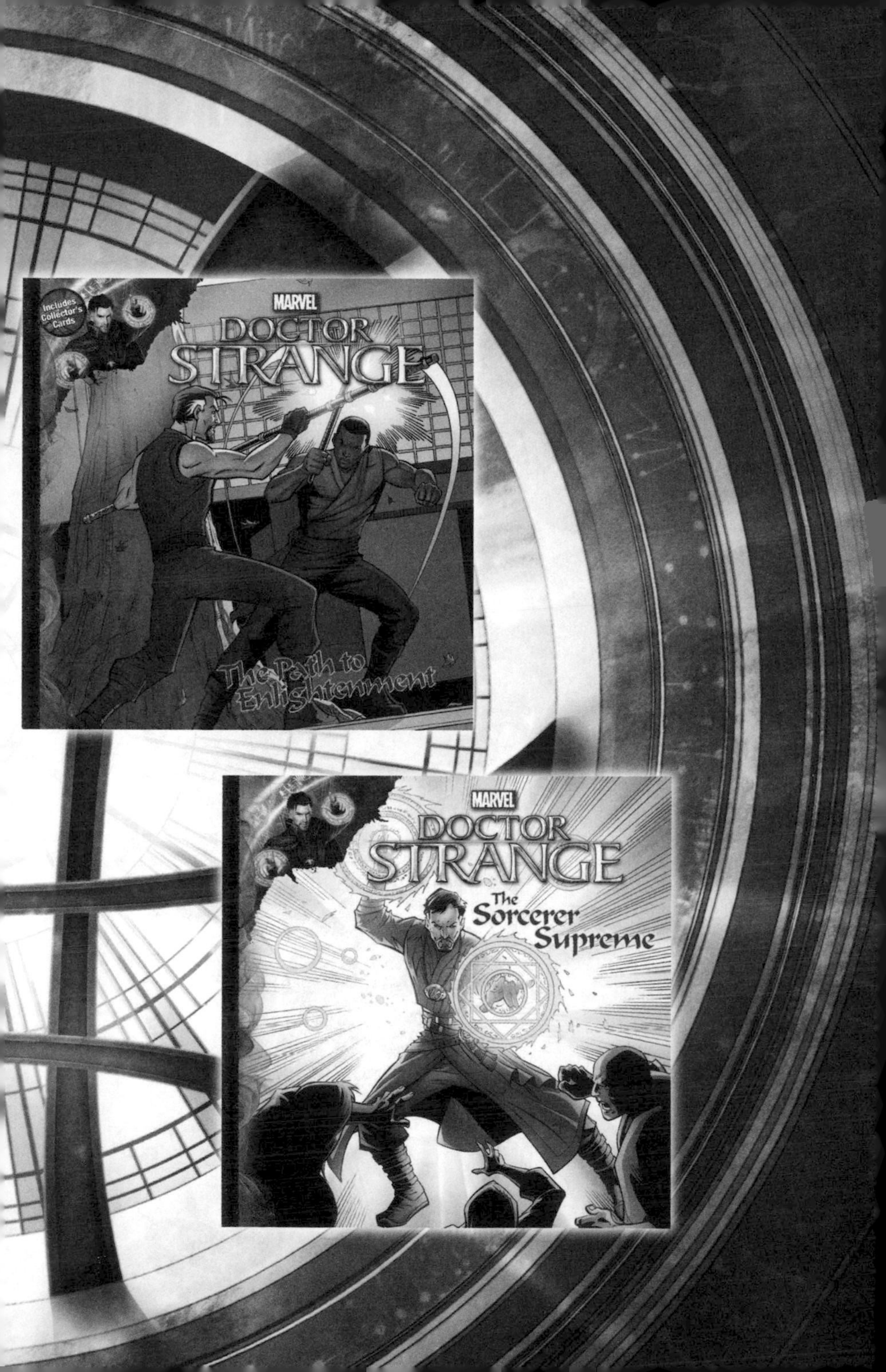

Includes Collector's Cards
MARVEL
DOCTOR STRANGE
The Path to Enlightenment
MARVEL
DOCTOR STRANGE
The Sorcerer Supreme

MORE SHIELD! MORE IRON! MORE MUSCLE! MORE HAMMER!

READ THEM ALL!

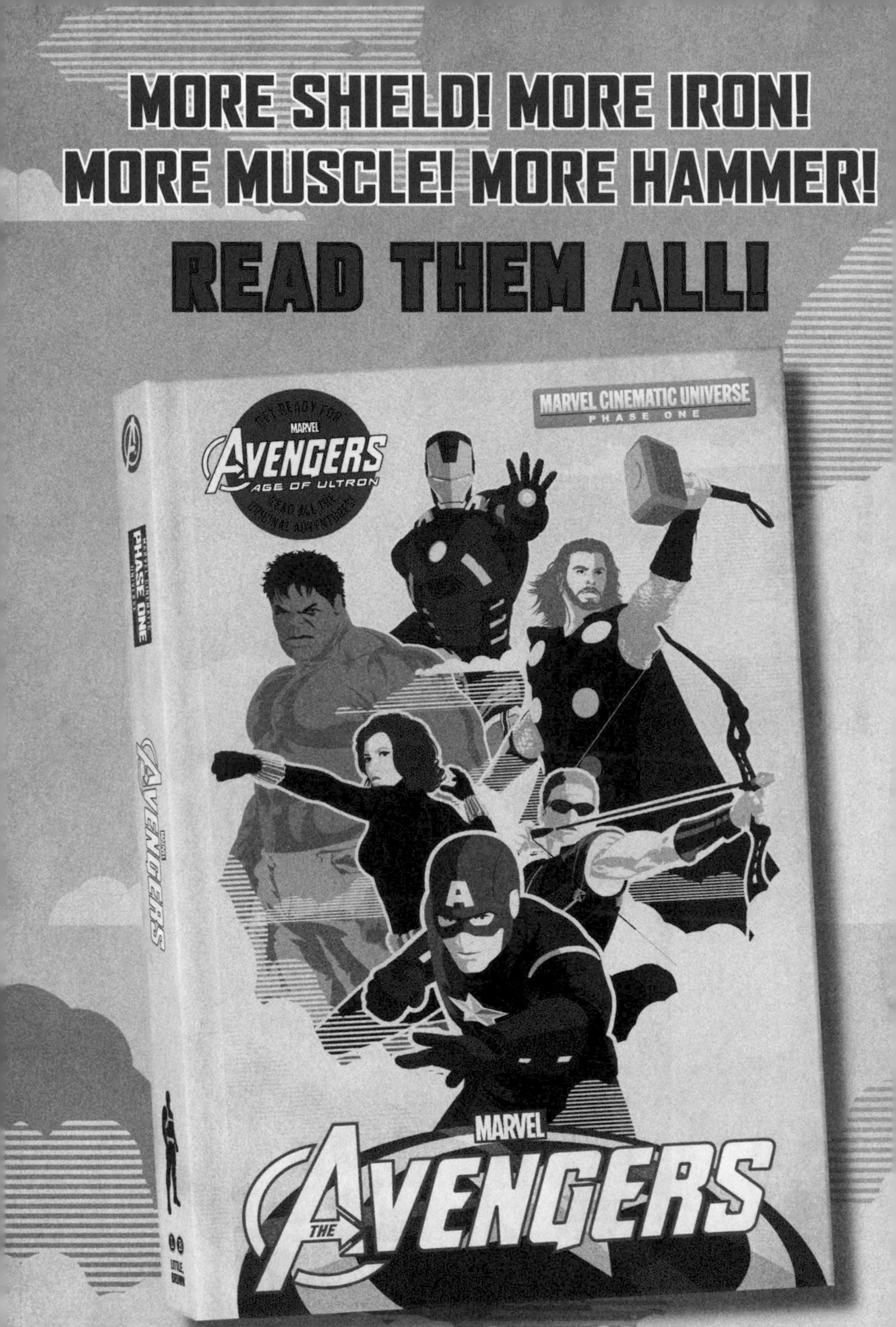
MARVEL CINEMATIC UNIVERSE
PHASE ONE
GET READY FOR
MARVEL
AVENGERS
AGE OF ULTRON
READ ALL THE ORIGINAL ADVENTURES
MARVEL
THE AVENGERS
LITTLE, BROWN

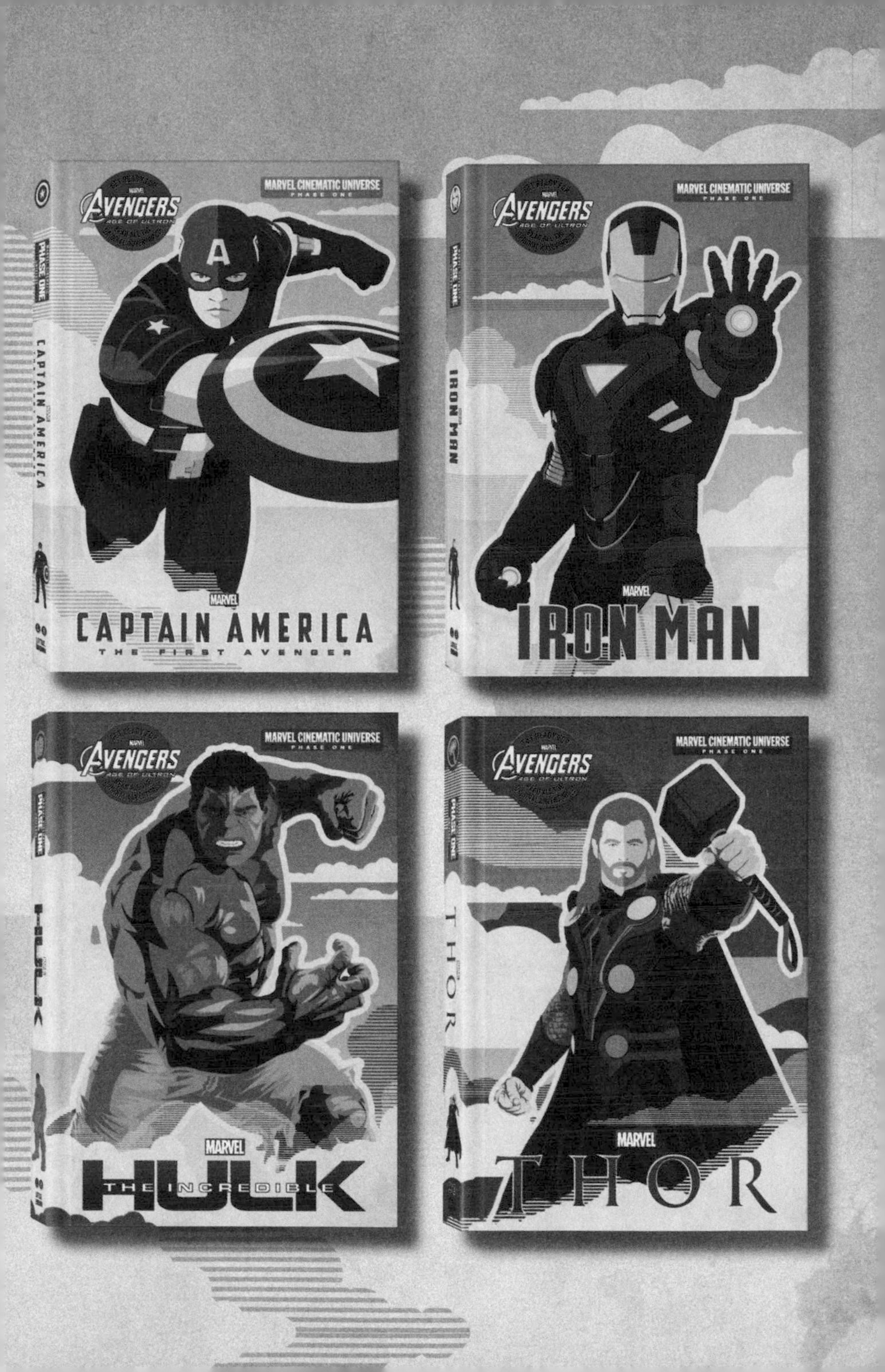
MARVEL CINEMATIC UNIVERSE
PHASE ONE
AVENGERS
AGE OF ULTRON
MARVEL
CAPTAIN AMERICA
THE FIRST AVENGER
MARVEL CINEMATIC UNIVERSE
PHASE ONE
AVENGERS
AGE OF ULTRON
MARVEL
IRON MAN
MARVEL CINEMATIC UNIVERSE
PHASE ONE
AVENGERS
AGE OF ULTRON
MARVEL
THE INCREDIBLE
HULK
MARVEL CINEMATIC UNIVERSE
PHASE ONE
AVENGERS
AGE OF ULTRON
MARVEL
THOR

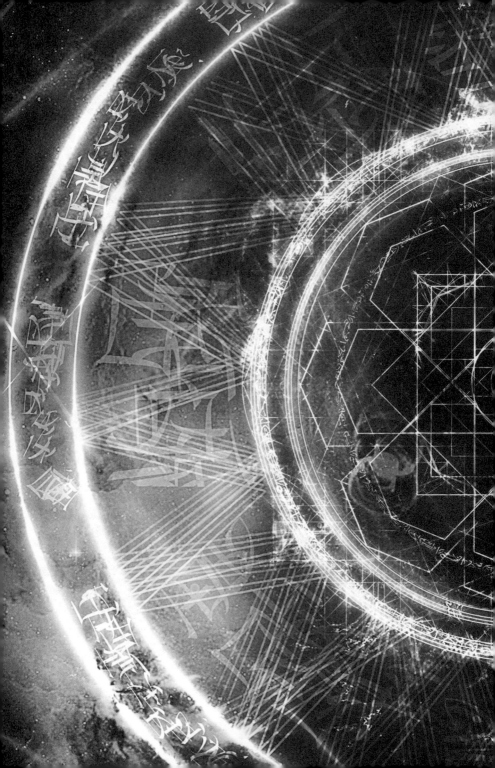